The Three Mrs. Monroes Trilogy

I0636161

Amelia
book one

by
Bernadette Marie

Bernadette Marie and 5 Prince Publishing
copyright 2014

This is a fictional work. The names, characters, incidents, places, and locations are solely the concepts and products of the author's imagination or are used to create a fictitious story and should not be construed as real.

5 PRINCE PUBLISHING AND BOOKS, LLC
PO Box 16507
Denver, CO 80216
www.5PrinceBooks.com

ISBN 13: 978-1-63112-038 ISBN 10: 1631120387
AMELIA
Bernadette Marie
Copyright Bernadette Marie 2014
Published by 5 Prince Publishing

Front Cover Viola Estrella

First Edition/First Printing July 2014 Printed U.S.A.

5 PRINCE PUBLISHING AND BOOKS, LLC.

To Stan,
You're always the man behind the woman when I need you to be—
usually holding me up when I think it would be easier to fall.

Acknowledgements

To Stan and our boys who delight me everyday and give me reason to climb out of bed and face the world. You are my power!

To Mom, Dad, and Sissy, you give me the base to every story I write—family. I believe that my power came from family.

To Connie, Clare, Marie, and Grace, you are the charge to my battery. Without you at my side perhaps I wouldn't have the strength to empower others to reach for their stars.

To June and Sara, it may have been books that brought us together and books that keep us engaged daily, but it is strength in sisterhood that keeps us together.

To my Street Team and Beta Readers, you are the food that feeds me and gives me strength. Without your encouragement the journey wouldn't be as much fun.

Dear Reader,

It's funny how an author's mind works. One day you wake up with this amazing idea for a book series and you begin to write. Then one day you pick up an old notebook from years ago and find that you planned the same book series back in the days you dreamed of being an author.

The Three Mrs. Monroes is one of those series I wrote down years ago. I'm so excited that now I can bring the stories of Amelia, Penelope, and Vivian to you as I always had planned.

Amelia is a strong woman. Raised by her father and her military mother, she knows a thing or two about being strong bodied and minded.

Sam Jackson is more brainy than brawny, but he knows when a woman is the right one and nothing can scare him away.

Of course a strong woman needs strong friends and that is what Amelia finds when she shows up at her husband's funeral and there are two more Mrs. Monroes.

I hope you enjoy the story and the sneak peak at Penelope.

Happy Reading,
Bernadette Marie

Amelia

Chapter One

God she was miserable

Amelia Monroe rolled up the window on her Ford Blazer as she turned down the dirt road which led to the small church. She'd only been to Parson's Gulch, Oklahoma once, and she certainly hadn't been privy to its back roads.

No, her husband Adam didn't want anything to do with the small town—and now she knew why.

She pulled into the lot of the small church and her heart began to race and a pain in her chest forced her to suck in a deep breath. She'd filed for divorce three months ago. Adam Monroe had lied to her for two years. There had been so much more to him and she'd failed to see it.

Now she sat in her truck, the heat suffocating her, as she watched his other wife and their two children climb from the black limousine and walk into the church.

The bastard had been married, with a family, long before he and Amelia had met. That was the end of her marriage. In that moment, she'd even contemplated killing him, but that wasn't how she did things—she was just angry.

Amelia Monroe had been raised to think calmly and use her words to fight, not her hands—though she could. She was plenty capable of killing the man. She was a trained martial artist. There were hundreds of ways she could have taken him down.

There had been no need to do that though. A land mine in Iraq had ended his life.

She sucked back tears as she thought about it. Damn it, he might have been a bastard, but she'd loved him. His death wasn't what she'd wanted—not really anyway.

She'd just wanted him to suffer for his lies and his deceptions. She didn't want him to be taken from his children—now that she knew he had them.

But here she was at the funeral of her husband and she'd opted to not be singled out. There would be no front pew in the church. She didn't want a flag or a limo. It would be better off if no one knew she was here.

She'd made the trek for peace of mind and, well, he was her husband. The fact that the attorney wanted to meet with her and Adam's other wife after the funeral also had pushed her to attend. After all, there was a lot to sort out.

Well, Amelia wasn't one to run. She'd hold her chin high and she'd face the woman Adam had lied to first. The children were only four and two. She wouldn't do anything to upset them. There wasn't a need for it. Besides, she knew one thing that the other woman didn't. The day was only going to get worse.

In the front pew of the church sat Adam's *first* wife, her children and what Amelia would assume were her parents. On the other side were his parents.

She'd never met them, but she recognized them from pictures. In fact, only until five months ago she was under the impression they were both dead.

She took a deep breath and let it out slowly as she sat down in the back pew of the church.

A man in a gray tailored suit stood at the end of the pew. "Are you Amelia?"

She held her breath. This wasn't what she wanted. She didn't want anyone to know who she was. With a slow nod she acknowledged that she was indeed Amelia.

"Sam Jackson, Adam's attorney."

AMELIA

The man extended his hand and she shook it. The tension in her shoulders began to slide away. At least this man carried as many secrets with him as she did.

"Do you mind if I sit with you? I don't know anyone else."

Amelia moved over and Sam sat down next to her. "You don't know Vivian?" she whispered and nodded toward Adam's other wife.

"No. My business with Adam was mostly done in Oklahoma City. I never met his wife. Wives." He gritted his teeth. "Sorry."

Amelia clasped her hands in her lap. "Not as sorry as I am."

The small church had filled. The mourners were obviously from the community and had probably known Adam since he was a child. Many had gone to the front and hugged his mother and Vivian. The children, one on each side, stayed close to her.

As the pastor spoke to the congregation, Amelia's eyes were glued to the casket draped with an American flag. She hadn't seen Adam in months. The last time they'd spoken, they'd fought. She'd told him she'd wanted a divorce and he argued with her over it. He said it had all been a big mistake, but she knew that was a lie.

Oh, she'd hoped he'd pay for what he did. This, however, wasn't what she'd had in mind.

She lowered her head and wiped her hand across her forehead.

Sam bent his head down. "Are you alright?"

She nodded. "I'm fine. It's just a bit warm in here."

The funeral was almost over when another woman walked through the door. She looked frazzled as if she'd taken that first dirt road and not the second, which Amelia had been warned about.

She'd been crying—a lot. Sam nodded to Amelia to scoot down and then signaled to the woman to sit next to him. She finally did so.

Amelia looked over at the woman who now was sobbing uncontrollably. She'd like to have cried over him like that too. Wasn't the widow of a man supposed to be in the front row of the church? Wasn't the widow of a U.S. solider supposed to know that she'd married an honorable man? Wasn't...

She let out a long breath as the pastor walked toward Adam's other wife and gave *her* a hug.

There was no reason to cause a scene. Sam was Adam's attorney. He was the only reason Amelia had made the trip. Obviously, Adam thought enough to have left her something and that's why she was here.

She wasn't one to point fingers and make others mad, that was why she'd asked for a divorce. She wasn't the kind of woman to show up on Vivian Monroe's doorstep and tell her that her husband of ten years had been married to her for two years. What good would that have done for his children?

Amelia watched as Vivian's daughter clung to her and her other daughter was held by her grandfather. Anger was quickly creeping into the areas that mourning hadn't filled. How could Adam have done this to his *children*?

The pall bearers stood as the pastor began to walk down the aisle. They carried the casket in a procession and his wife, children, and family followed.

As Vivian reached the back of the church she turned her head and gave Amelia a very knowing glance. One that said *you don't belong here.*

Sam touched her arm. "Are you sure you're okay?"

"I wish you wouldn't have asked me to be here."

"I appreciate it," he said as the woman next to him began to sob even harder.

Sam turned to her. "Ma'am, are you going to be okay?"

The woman, with her blonde curls bouncing every time she tried to suck in a breath, shook her head. "Was that his wife? His *other* wife?"

Amelia felt a pain shoot through her chest. She leaned across, in front of Sam as the other mourners left the church, and looked the woman in her bloodshot eyes.

"Are you Penelope?" she asked through gritted teeth and the woman slowly nodded.

Amelia sat back against the pew as the church emptied out and crossed her arms over her chest.

The first Mrs. Monroe had escorted her husband out of the church.

The second Mrs. Monroe was hidden in the back, as if she hadn't existed.

And the third Mrs. Monroe had walked in late.

Chapter Two

Sam wondered if he would suffocate from the thick air between the three of them. He hadn't expected Penelope to show up. In fact, he hadn't even talked to the woman yet, but someone had.

The latter Mrs. Monroe had only been Mrs. for a short two months. But she must have loved the S.O.B. he figured, or she wouldn't have married him.

He gave it more thought. Two months they'd been married, which meant that he'd only spent a few weeks with this bride. He'd been deployed for the past six weeks—shortly after the second Mrs. Monroe filed for divorce.

Sam shook his head. What was this guy's deal?

The church was now empty, except for him and the second and third Mrs. Monroes.

Amelia Monroe sat with her arms over her chest and her cheeks were bright red. Penelope Monroe sobbed and sobbed. He wondered if she'd run out of tears.

He swallowed hard. "Are either of you ladies headed to the cemetery?"

Simultaneously they both turned to him and he suddenly worried for his life.

Amelia let out a long breath, but her eyes were focused on Penelope. "I think I'll head back to my hotel. I will be in your office on Monday morning."

Sam nodded as Amelia stood.

Penelope pushed her shoulders back. "I hadn't thought this far ahead." She began to sob again. "I came to see him off, but I don't want to look at the faces of his children as they say goodbye to their father."

The tears came harder and Sam placed his arm around her shoulders. "You should just head back home or to your hotel." He looked up at Amelia who rolled her eyes.

Amelia brushed a loose strand of hair out of her eyes. "Do you have a place to stay?"

Penelope looked up at her and shook her head. "No. I didn't think about it. I spent my last paycheck to drive out here. Adam had never sent me money like he said he would. I lost my job. I don't..." she stopped talking and tried to catch her breath.

"I have a hotel room with two beds." Amelia dropped her shoulders. "You can stay with me."

Penelope sucked in a harsh breath. "Are you sure? There is no reason for you to be nice to me."

"Did you know about me?"

Penelope shook her head, again.

Amelia puckered her lips. "He was a good secret keeper. I'm not going to hold that against you personally."

Sam couldn't help the small smile that he felt on his lips. This woman was quite a force—a very attractive quality.

By her physique he knew she was strong. Not many women could boast a sleeveless blouse with defined shoulders and cut biceps like Amelia Monroe had.

Her dark hair was pulled back from her neck, which he didn't blame her for. That church was hot as hell.

She had her nails done and there was a pink shimmer to her lips. So even though she was as strong as a man a feminine vibe still resonated from her.

Sam pulled a card from his pocket and handed it to Penelope.

"I'm Adam's attorney. If you need anything you can call me."

"Why are you two so nice to me?"

AMELIA

Amelia exchanged glances with Sam. This Mrs. Monroe was going to be some work, he could tell.

It had taken another twenty minutes for them to calm Penelope down so that she could drive. When they finally got her outside and into her car, Amelia convinced her to take a ten minute power nap with the air conditioner running. She'd seemed too out of sorts to drive.

They walked toward Sam's truck. "How did you know there was a third?"

"Wife?" she asked as she opened her door and threw her purse into the passenger seat.

Sam nodded.

"Asshole told me about her. Said I didn't need to worry about his happiness, he'd found happiness wrapped in a blonde beauty named Penelope. It wasn't until after he died that I found out that he'd married her too."

"Was this a game to him?" He didn't like the way it sounded, but Amelia didn't seem to be the type to wince at words.

"I've never known anyone in such a position. I don't even care about me. Two years of my life wasted, but hell, he wasn't around for most of it anyway. I thought he was on duty most the time. I didn't know some of that time he was home with his family."

Sam reached out and touched her hand. "I'm truly sorry for your loss."

"I appreciate that." Amelia looked over at Penelope's car. "She's going to be harder to convince to move on. I moved on months ago. I'm not going to let Adam Monroe ruin the rest of my life."

He opened the door to his truck. "You have a good attitude."

"I'll have a better one when this is over. I'm over at the Holiday Inn if you need me before Monday."

"Thanks."

She started toward Penelope's car and then looked back at Sam. "You don't know a good steak place around here do you?"

He laughed. "There's one off the highway about two miles from where you're staying."

"Something tells me I'm going to have to leave this one sobbing in the room. I'll need a drink and a steak."

"That sounds good."

She narrowed her eyes at him. "You married?"

"No. Never have been."

She nodded slowly. "Interested in accompanying a non-grieving widow to dinner? I'm guessing I'll need some decent conversation by tonight."

Sam wasn't sure how long he'd stood there contemplating what had just been said. Had he just been asked out by one of Adam Monroe's widows—at his funeral?

No, he'd been asked to keep her company.

What had gotten into him?

"I could go for a steak. I could pick you up at seven."

She shook her head. "I'll meet you there at seven."

Sam agreed with a wave, got into his truck, and drove away as she woke up Penelope.

As he pulled onto the long dirt road, he looked into his rearview mirror. She might have a hard outside, but he could see the care she was taking with Penelope. There was compassion in that one that didn't come out too often he figured.

The evening should prove to be eventful.

Sam waited in his truck outside the steak house. He'd arrived ten minutes early and he saw her truck drive in ten minutes late.

Amelia Monroe was one to do things on her terms.

He stepped out of the truck and headed toward her before she turned off the engine. He was reaching for her door when she flung it open, narrowly missing his hand.

"Oops. Did I get ya?" She stepped out and shut the door with her hip.

She had changed into a pair of jeans which rode low on her hips and as she walked a step in front of him to clear the back end of the truck he noticed she had a tattoo peeking out of the waistband. Her fitted T-shirt hid the top part.

"So have you ever eaten here before?" She asked as he caught up to her.

"No. Just saw it on the way in yesterday."

"I hope they have some good beer. I need a drink."

He opened the door for her to pass through. "When I think of having a drink I think of something a little harder than beer."

"Not me. Beer is good."

The hostess sat them in a corner booth. She took the side that faced the door.

In all his years of representing people, he'd learned to read them. She was cautious. If her back was to the door, she'd forever be turning to see who was coming after her.

Their waiter came to the table as soon as they sat down.

"I'll have a Blue Moon," she quickly ordered.

"I'll have the same," Sam added. He watched her casually pick up her menu and scan over it. "How was your afternoon? Did Penelope calm down?"

"She finally fell asleep about an hour before I left." She set her menu down and looked at him. "I usually run out of tears in an hour. This one produces them by the bucket."

He smiled. "Loss affects people differently."

"I suppose." She picked up her menu again.

"How are you doing?"

She set the menu down again and leaned in on her elbows. "The guy screwed me over completely. I married a married family man and the moment I found out I dumped his ass. And before the divorce papers are filed, he's got another wife. I'm not mourning the loss of my marriage, like Penelope and Vivian are. I'm mourning the loss of two good years I can't get back. But I'll make up for them. You can count on that." She sat back against the booth and crossed her arms over her chest. "The world lost a good soldier though. He could aim a gun, disarm a bomb, and his number of saves outnumbers his kills. I hope they recognize that, even if he was a dick."

He didn't mean to chuckle, but he had. He liked her feistiness.

The waiter returned and collected their order. There was no surprise to him when she ordered her steak medium rare, but more on the mooing side.

When their beers arrived, with the customary orange slice balanced on the rim, she took the orange and squeezed it into the beer, then floated it inside.

Sam took his orange off and set it to the side.

"You tossing that?" She made a motion to the discarded orange.

"Yes."

"Mind?" She reached for it and did the same thing with his orange as she'd done with hers.

"So how did you meet Adam?"

Amelia took a sip of her beer and then set it down. An enormous smile crossed her lips.

"I kicked his ass."

The answer wasn't what he'd expected as he took a sip of his beer. It was all he could do not to spit it back out.

"What do you mean?"

"That's how we met. I'm a martial artist. Third degree black belt. I was helping my instructor, a sixth degree grand master, teach a self-defense class on base for the wives of soldiers. My thought was it would help them protect themselves from their husbands. These guys are trained men that women can't stand up to. They go through shit you'll never see. Sometimes they snap. A woman has to be prepared.

"Well, he'd volunteered to be an attacker. He had a cocky grin on his face from the first moment he looked at me. He came at me to attack and I laid him flat. Sucker was a goner. He fell in love with me the moment his vision cleared and he could breathe again."

Sam was beginning to understand the allure to her.

He didn't particularly like aggressive women. He'd never been too successful when it came to them responding to his more sensitive side. It wasn't hard to assume that Amelia would be the same. She'd eat him up and spit him out.

"How long did you date before you got married?"

She snorted a laugh and then sipped her beer. "I had him in bed by the second day of training. He came back to visit me a week later, when he got back to town. We eloped in Vegas two weeks after that."

"Never a clue that something was up with him?"

"Not a one. But he was trained to keep secrets and execute maneuvers that no one saw coming. It carried over into his personal life."

"I take it you're going to be the calm one in my office."

"Oh, I'll be calm. This isn't my fault. It's none of our faults. I can't imagine why he felt he needed to do this to people."

The waiter delivered their dinner and Amelia picked up her fork and knife and started digging in.

Sam couldn't help but watch and admire. Oh, the last few women he'd taken out were so dainty. He liked this aggressiveness to everything—even dinner.

It was hard to remind himself that she'd buried her husband that morning.

She took a bite of steak and pointed at him with her fork. "What do you know about the other two?"

"I'm not sure I should share my knowledge."

She shrugged. "I get it. Client stuff."

"Yes. Client stuff."

She took another bite. "This is what kills me." She swallowed. "I'm nothing like either of them. Vivian looks like the perfect little house wife. Penelope, though I'm sure she's a sweet girl, I don't think she has a brain in her head."

"Maybe together you made the perfect woman." He was afraid the moment it came out it was going to go the wrong way.

She shrugged. "Maybe."

"So when you're not kicking the asses of soldiers, what do you do?"

"For a living?" she asked as she took another bite of steak.

He nodded.

"I teach martial arts three days a week. The rest of the time I'm a personal trainer."

"As in you work in a gym and build bodies?"

She laughed as she took a sip from her beer. "Yeah, I train bodies."

"Do you compete?"

"No. You will not find me strutting along in some clear heels showing off and being judged."

He liked her even more now and he wondered who would ever stand up to this woman and judge her?

"So where is home to you?"

"Now I live in Georgia, but originally I'm from Oklahoma City."

"Really?"

"That's kinda what got me in bed with Adam in the first place. We had a hometown connection. Or home area connection that is."

"I see."

"Are you originally from Oklahoma too?"

"Yes," he said as he took a drink of his beer.

"Hmmm, looks like we connect too." She wiggled her eyebrows at him and he nearly choked on his drink.

She laughed.

"Sorry. I'm a bit forward."

He cleared his throat. "It's fine. I just…"

"Didn't expect to be hit on by a woman who just attended the funeral of her husband?"

"Yes."

"Well," she lifted her glass in a toast. "I hope he finds an angel to hit on. This angel has moved on."

"You don't feel bad?"

"Sure I do. But in two years I've only spent maybe thirteen months with my husband here and there. I filed for divorce three months ago. He was deployed for most of that. It's not like he was a constant in my life."

He understood that, which in itself confused him. Why did he want to understand it?

But when he looked at her he couldn't help himself. There was a lot to this woman and he couldn't help but wonder if he was man enough to find out all about her.

Amelia continued her assault on her steak, washing down every other bite with her beer. When the waiter came back to the table she ordered another beer and a meal to go.

"That girl is going to wake up and be ravenous," she said as she finished her beer, ordered another, and the waiter set the other in front of her.

"I don't get it. Why do you want to take care of her? You don't owe her anything."

"She deserves some respect. I don't think she's used to getting any."

He rested his chin on his hand and his elbow on the table. "You're a good judge of character, aren't you?"

"Always thought I was, until Adam." She filled her fork with a bit of potato and then held it as though she was having second thoughts about the bite. Finally she took the bite and quickly rinsed it down with the beer. Then she pushed her plate away and rested her arms on the table.

"You know, I'm not even going to second guess Adam. He was a fine soldier. One of the best I've ever worked with. And damn, he was fine in bed."

Sam could feel the heat in his cheeks, but he tried to keep composed.

Amelia tapped her fingers on the table. "He was a good man. He just really screwed up when it came to women."

"You could say that."

"And hell, if I fell that hard for him, I don't blame Penelope for doing it too. He was one fine man to look at."

Hearing her talk about him, Sam was beginning to feel extremely unmasculine altogether.

Amelia sat back in her seat. "Something tells me Penelope needs a friend, and quite frankly I'm in the market for a few myself. We have some common bond. I'll give her a fair chance."

Sam smiled. He probably looked awkward and nerdy, but at this moment he just didn't care. "I like you. You make me look at things differently. I'm supposed to be objective, as a lawyer, but I don't see things like you do."

"My life is going to go on and so is hers. Hell, I'd be friends with Vivian too, but I'm sure that ship will sail after Monday."

He swallowed hard. He was sure it would too. Sometimes is sucked knowing all the secrets.

Amelia leaned in on her arms again and moved closer toward Sam across the table.

"So, lawyer man. Tell me about you. What makes you tick?"

At that very moment the answer was her. He was wrapped up in this woman. She was like no one he'd ever met, nor could he imagine he'd meet someone like her again. Certainly they broke the mold after they made her.

Sam bit down on his lip. "There isn't much to tell. I draw up wills, help set up trust funds, supervise estates. Every once in a while I handle a divorce."

"Can you run?"

Sam narrowed his gaze on her. "Run?"

"Yeah. Do you own some running shoes?"

He had to think. They were tucked in his closet, back behind the vacuum cleaner, which he should probably drag out and use too. "Yeah, I have a pair."

"What do you say you meet me for a run tomorrow? There's a lake just about twenty minutes from my hotel. My guess is it's about half way between your place and mine."

"The lake at Derby Park?"

She grinned. "Yeah, I think that's the one. Has a dinosaur on the playground?"

"That would be it."

The waiter set the take out box on the table and the check rested atop the box. She was quick to snatch it up and start fishing her credit card from her small wallet purse.

Sam went for his wallet in his pocket and she waved him off. "I got this. You get breakfast tomorrow."

He eased back in his seat. "O-kay."

She handed the card to the waiter and then turned her eyes back on him. "I make you uneasy don't I?"

"Let's just say I've never met a woman like you."

"Not the first time I've heard that. I won't bite you. I promise."

He nodded like an idiot and she smiled wider, leaning in closer over the table.

"I only bite if you ask me to," she said with a wink and then sat back when the waiter brought the credit card slip and a pen.

Amelia tucked the credit card back into her purse and stood, grabbing the food box off the table. "Seven o'clock. I'll meet you at the lake."

Sam just nodded as she walked out of the restaurant. God he was in serious trouble. He couldn't run.

Chapter Three

Amelia opened the door to the room quietly, but there had been no need. Penelope was sitting propped up on the bed watching TV.

"I brought you something to eat."

Penelope crinkled up her nose. "Thank you. I'm not feeling too well right now."

Amelia nodded. "I'll tuck it in the mini-fridge and you can eat it later if you want."

"Thank you."

She walked over to the small fridge and set the box inside. With a glance at the clock she realized it was only nine o'clock and she was exhausted. Usually she could keep going until eleven or later, but today had drained her. Although, that quirky little lawyer man was quite enjoyable.

Then the thought hit her. He probably thought she was some kind of crazy slut asking him to dinner like that.

When had anyone's opinion of her ever mattered? She kicked off her shoes and headed toward the small bathroom.

Adam wasn't her husband. Nope, she couldn't even consider him that. They'd rolled in the sack and had one hell of a good time. The cheap gold band on her finger was as worthless as the marriage had been. Besides, she'd divorced him. His death signed that paper. It was okay to look at other men. He'd obviously not taken their vows seriously.

But it ached in her chest. Why wasn't she worthy of a man who would treat her like a woman? Just because she was stronger than most men—that made them fear her or want to take advantage of her?

Screw that. No one was going to get into her head like that. Adam Monroe was the messed up one. Not her. She turned on the water to the shower and let it warm.

There were some very cute qualities to Sam Jackson.

She picked up the brush on the counter and pulled it through her hair. Cute? When did she ever think *cute* was a quality? Dear Lord, she was losing her freaking mind.

Tomorrow she was going to get to the lake an hour earlier than Sam and run until she passed out. And then she'd run him around that lake, if he in fact could run.

Maybe she'd then get it through her thick skull that she was in Parson's Gulch because her husband wasn't an upstanding man—and dead. And maybe, just maybe, she'd realize this wasn't where she wanted to stay and that Sam Jackson had only been a nice distraction on what could have been—should have been—the worst day of her life.

Just as she lifted the hem of her shirt to pull it off, there was a knock at the door.

"Can I come in? I don't feel good." Penelope's voice shook as she spoke.

Amelia quickly opened the door and Penelope rushed through and straight to the toilet where she threw up whatever she might have eaten for breakfast, because Amelia was sure she hadn't had lunch.

She winced at the sound and walked out into the main room.

Great. Not only was she sharing her room, which she hadn't planned on, but now her co-wife roommate was sick. This was seriously proving to be the worst week of her life.

Penelope stumbled out of the bathroom, a washcloth pressed to her mouth. Her face was pale and her eyes watered.

"Are you okay?" Amelia thought the question was as dumb as it sounded. No, she wasn't alright, but she'd had to ask.

"I'll be fine. Thank you." Penelope walked back to her bed and lay down. "I'm sorry to be such a problem."

"It's fine. We're all having an off week."

Penelope didn't have a retort, she only moaned.

"I'll leave the door unlocked in case you need in," Amelia said as she hurried back to the bathroom to partake in what would be, more than likely, just a lukewarm shower.

The rest of the night had been fairly quiet. Amelia was sure that Penelope might have gotten up one time during the night to get sick, but she hadn't awakened her, so Amelia counted it as good.

The Oklahoma sun had already risen by the time she made it to the lake at six o'clock. And it was already hot. The thought crossed her mind that she didn't really belong anywhere anymore. Oklahoma might have been her home, and Georgia where she'd set down her own roots, but maybe it was time for a change. Did it get blistering hot in Montana? Winters might be brutal, but that's what long underwear and coats were for. But six in the morning and eighty-nine degrees wasn't going to cut it much longer. By two in the afternoon the July heat would be well into the hundreds. What fun was that?

Amelia tightened up the hot pink laces on her neon yellow running shoes and started around the lake.

Sam rested the two Starbucks cups on the hood of his truck and then leaned up against the vehicle. She'd said seven, right? It was six-fifty in the morning and she was already half way around the lake. Maybe she'd be too tired to run again, or so he hoped. That was some of the thought behind the cups of coffee. He'd never usually spend that kind of money on the drink, but he was desperately trying to persuade her to not make him run.

Yesterday, sure he thought he might get in a lap, but when he was winded after having moved the vacuum to find the shoes, he thought better of it.

Ten minutes later she was headed toward him, her hand cupped around the back of her head as she sucked in the heat of the morning.

Her sunglasses shielded her eyes, but the smile did something to him he wasn't sure he should admit, even to himself.

The body which was exposed around running shorts and a tank top was pure muscle. There were defining lines each time she took a step. She could crush him with just a well pointed finger to his chest, that he was sure of.

"You look a bit too cozy for a run," she joked as she neared him.

"Do I? I brought you a coffee." He handed her the cup. "It's straight up black. I didn't know what you might like."

"You pegged me just right."

She blew a breath through the small hole in the lid and then took a sip.

Sam picked up his cup and did the same. "You did say seven, right? I'm not late am I?"

She laughed easily and then wiped away a bead of sweat from her brow with the back of her hand. "No. I was restless so I got here at six to run."

"You must be pretty tired then." *Please be too tired.*

She laughed again. "I've got another hour in me. But I'm thinking you brought coffee as a deterrent."

"I'm transparent, huh?"

"Just a bit." She walked around him and leaned against the truck next to him. "So you're not a runner?"

"Had to dust off the shoes."

"You're in great shape for not exercising."

Sam cleared his throat. "Yoga."

She grinned behind her cup. "Probably eases the mind of a lawyer."

He lifted his cup, as if in salute. "That it does."

"Well," she sipped again, "I guess that just leaves breakfast. Tell me you know a good place to eat."

"That I can do."

Amelia followed him up the highway to a spot he'd grown very familiar with over time, Chunky Pete's. When she climbed out of her truck she was already laughing.

"The name makes me want to go back to the lake and run more."

"If you have a cinnamon roll you'll have to."

She lifted her brows high above the rim of her aviator glasses. "I just might have to have one then."

And she did.

Sam loved watching her eat. Last night it was the steak and this morning she was assaulting a cinnamon roll. Well, she wasn't like other women. She wasn't afraid it would land on her hips. She enjoyed it and then would take care of it later. The thought stuck. He knew just enough about her to know she liked men the same.

"So how come you never got married?" she asked as she bit off another piece of her roll.

"Women got on my nerves too quickly." That didn't sound right. "I don't go for men."

She must have understood his concern. "So you never found the right woman?"

"Yeah."

"Women get on my nerves too. Whiney. Cry baby. You name it and I just want to throw them to the ground." She washed down the roll with her coffee. "I guess that's why I train them to be tough. I can't stand when they can't take care of themselves."

"You seem very efficient in that department."

She nodded slowly. "That's how I was raised."

It was intriguing. Did he dare ask? "Did you have only brothers?"

"Two sisters and we were military brats."

"Your dad was in the service?"

Her lips curled into a grin. "Mom."

Again, he hadn't expected that.

She sat back in her chair. "My mother the drill sergeant. My dad was years ahead of his time. He was a stay-at-home dad."

"Not so uncommon now, right?"

"He saw us to the bus, made our lunches, and even hemmed our pants. Mom took charge of the house, meaning it was done to her liking. Things were a bit more at ease when she was deployed, but otherwise we all walked the line, even Dad."

Sam lifted his mug in salute. "Your dad did a fine job."

"Thank you."

"What branch?"

"Army." She looked down at her plate and then pushed it away. "Sniper got her in Desert Storm."

Sam could feel the blood drain from his face. "You couldn't have been very old."

"It was where she'd wanted to be. I can't be sad. My dad finished raising us. We were trained to be tough and stand on our own two feet. He remarried when I graduated high school and he moved to Florida."

"You're the baby."

"They'd never call me that."

There was a glimmer in her eye that told him they might have tried and they didn't get away with it.

"Had you and Adam planned to have a family?"

She shook her head. "No. That never came up. Now I know why."

"But did you want kids?"

"No. Not my style." She tapped her fingers on the table. "What about you? Can't find the right woman, but did you ever want a family?"

Sam thought about it for a moment. "I suppose I did. I came from a good family. No reason not to want one."

She grinned. "You don't sound too convincing."

He laughed. "I think it would be easier to answer if I had the right woman in my life."

Silence settled between them. She watched the people come and go in the diner and he watched her.

She was spinning her fork on the table and she was so strong her muscles flexed with each movement. He knew if he asked about anyone in that restaurant she'd be able to tell him all about them. She'd been observing since she'd walked in the door—something he knew she was trained to do.

"Are you ready for the meeting Monday?" He asked as he lifted his coffee mug to his lips only to be disappointed that the brown liquid had gone cold. Where was that waitress?

"Sure. You don't know what his will says do you?"

This was a tricky conversation, but he could answer her honestly. "I know he changed his will before he was deployed again. It was sent to me from Iraq. I haven't opened it."

"Element of surprise?"

Something like that. He knew he'd be seeing Amelia, the last thing he'd wanted was to slip up and say anything. "Surprises are good."

She snorted a laugh. "Sure they are when your parents buy you the one thing you wanted for your birthday. Not so much when you find out your husband has been cheating on you. It's even worse when you find out he's been cheating on his wife *with* you."

"I'm sorry. That was insensitive."

She brushed away his comment with her hand in the air. "It's nothing. I'm thinking everything happens for a reason. There is a reason he wasn't faithful to Vivian, though I can't imagine why. And he and I fought, a lot."

"So why stay?"

"The making up was worth it."

Right. Women thought that way too, sometimes.

She adjusted her head from side to side as if to work out the tension in her neck. "I don't even know if Penelope was a surprise really. I think we were a surprise to her. But I think there is more to her. There's something she's not telling me, aside from the fact that she's so nervous she's sick."

"She's sick?"

"Yeah. The heat, travel, emotions, everything got to her. She was up all night. I'm going to get her a little something and take it back."

Did she even realize she was so sensitive? "You're being very nice to her."

"She didn't ask for this. None of us did."

"So do you plan to head back after the meeting?"

She shrugged. "Yeah, I suppose. Nothing left here in Oklahoma for me."

"Right." *Right?* What had he expected? Why did he care?

"Nothing left in Georgia either." Her gaze had lowered to her hands on the table.

"Time for a change?"

"I'd been considering that."

"Maybe that'll work out for you then."

She sighed—actually sighed. "Yeah, maybe it will."

Chapter Four

Amelia set the bag of food on the table and looked around the small motel room. Penelope was in the bathroom, in the shower. She certainly hoped she didn't startle easily. If Amelia were to have come out of the bathroom and someone was in the room they might get the crap beat out of them. She was sure Penelope wasn't going to be harmful to her.

She turned on the TV, hoping that the sound would alert Penelope that she was there. An old Friends episode was on so she sat down on the bed, laid back and watched.

It was one of those episodes where Ross kept trying to convince Rachel that it was okay to sleep with someone else since they were *on a break*. She chuckled to herself. Was that what Adam had in mind when he kept taking wives?

The door to the bathroom opened and Penelope stepped out, followed by a room full of steam.

"Feeling any better?" Amelia asked.

"Not really."

"Well, I brought you some food. I figured you'd need something to eat."

"Thanks."

Penelope pulled a sundress out of her suitcase, stepped around the corner, and came back into the room with it on and the towel now wrapped around her hair.

Her skin was pale and there were dark circles under her eyes. Amelia felt horrible for her. She supposed if she'd found out about Vivian only a few months after she'd married Adam she'd have looked just as bad.

Well, that wasn't true. She figured she was a much different breed than the other two. If she'd have found out before she started to hate him she'd have kicked the crap out of him—or out of someone. She'd have tied one on and then taken one or two guys to bed. Yep, she was sure that wasn't how Vivian and Penelope worked.

Penelope seemed to keep it all inside. That didn't look healthy. Maybe she could convince her to hit the gym with her and she could teach her a few moves against the punching bag. They'd both feel better then.

"Is that what you brought me?" Penelope pointed to the bag.

"Yeah. I brought you a breakfast sandwich. I thought if you wanted to pick it apart it would have the most things to eat out of it."

Penelope laughed. "Thanks." She sat down at the small table and opened the sandwich. "You're very nice. I really didn't expect that."

"I do have a reputation."

Penelope's eyes opened wide. "That wasn't what I meant. I'm sorry."

"I'm just joking."

"Oh," she said softly as she pulled off a piece of the muffin and ate it. "I figured you and his other wife would meet me at the door and want to kill me. Really, I've even had dreams about it."

"Well, I could kill a person with my bare hands, but I wouldn't. Especially when it wasn't your fault that the man lied to all of us. He'd been doing that long before he drug you into this."

Penelope nodded and took another bite of the sandwich.

"The lawyer said I needed to be here. But I'm not sure I should be." She looked down at the food and back up at Amelia. "How could he do this to his kids?"

Amelia shrugged. "I don't know. Son-of-a-bitch will rot for that. Those kids will hate him now and before they might have thought he was a hero."

"I don't want them to hate him."

Yeah, Amelia didn't want them too either. "They're still young. They don't need to know about us." She sat up on the bed and planted her feet on the floor. "A far as I'm concerned we go to the meeting in Sam's office and then we go our different ways."

Penelope nodded. "Right. That would be the best idea." She looked at the food, pulled off another piece of the sandwich and then tossed it back into the bag. "You called him Sam. Do you know him?"

"Met him at the funeral. Good looking though, don't you think?"

Penelope shrugged. "I suppose."

"We had dinner last night and breakfast this morning. I guess tomorrow will be the last day I see him though." She chuckled. "But something tells me if I could just take him for a roll he has an animal buried inside."

Penelope's face scrunched up and then her eyes opened wide and her cheeks colored pink. "Oh!"

Amelia laughed. "I'm not much of a prude. Sorry if I offend you."

"No. No offense taken." Penelope grinned. "I wish I was more like you."

"Men use women for sex all the time. I don't see why we can't use them a little too."

Penelope bit down on her lip. "I'd never thought that way before. Adam was my..." she stopped talking and Amelia just watched her.

The moment the reality hit her she got to her feet. "You were a virgin?"

Penelope's lips pursed. "It's not that uncommon you know. Some people wait until they are married."

"Holy shit!" Amelia laughed. "I think you're a saint."

A tear rolled down Penelope's cheek. "That was a lot of saving only to have him die."

This was the part Amelia didn't do so well with. What was she supposed to do with a blubbering girl? She did the only thing she knew to do—she patted her on the back.

Penelope's body shook as she sucked back a breath. "I'm sorry. I'm so sorry."

"Why? He screwed us all over. It's okay to be mad. I'm mad."

"I don't want to be mad. It's not good."

"Like hell it ain't." Amelia moved back toward the bed to sit down, but decided she needed to pace. "I'm pissed. I'm pissed that I fell in love with the guy and I'm pissed he was lying to me. He deserved the beating I gave him."

That made Penelope chuckle. "You hit him?"

"Hell yeah. Punched him right in the nose."

Penelope's chuckle grew into a laugh as she wiped away the last of her tears. "I think that was when I met him. He had a black eye and his nose was swollen."

"Great. I kicked his ass and he went out looking for a woman."

The humor left Penelope's face. "He took one of my friends home that night."

Now Amelia needed to sit down. "Are you kidding me?"

Penelope shook her head. "No. Now how dumb do I look?"

"As a species we are all dumb." And Amelia was feeling that way more now than she ever had. The extra wives were one thing. She'd come to grips with it, but now she knew there was casual cheating.

Anger boiled through her and she wished she'd have broken more than his nose.

Amelia took a deep breath. "What made you want to be with him? Especially if you knew about him taking girls home?"

The tears were back and Penelope let them fall. "I just fell in love with him. He was so handsome and talked to me so sweetly. And he waited for me. I mean, well you know."

"He didn't have sex with you until you were married?"

"Right."

Real upstanding guy, Amelia thought. "You deserve better."

Penelope looked down at the floor. She laced her fingers together and squeezed them until Amelia noticed they were going white.

"Hey," she stood and put her hand over Penelope's. "Calm down. We all make mistakes."

"I have to live with this one."

"We all do. But losing your virginity to some lying ass isn't the end of the…"

"I'm pregnant."

~*~

Amelia had done what she could to comfort Penelope. Finally she'd convinced her to lie down and rest. But admittedly that wasn't for Penelope. It was so Amelia could escape.

It was a good thing she still had on her running shoes because she didn't know how far she'd have to run before she unlocked her jaw and stopped gritting her teeth.

She was mad. Oh, she was pissed!

She was pissed that Adam had lied to her. Pissed that Adam had been so careless and stupid. Pissed that he died before their divorce was absolutely final. Hadn't she had his homecoming all planned out? She was pissed because she didn't get the last word in.

An hour and a half, or so, later she had run until she didn't even know where she was. There was a Walmart, a McDonald's, and a gas station, but hell if she could see her motel.

Sweat dripped down her neck, her cheeks, and from her hair. Her sunglasses were fogged over and she was finally out of steam.

She sat down on a bench outside the Walmart and sucked in the hot Oklahoma air. Her phone had exactly ten percent battery left.

Well, hell, she was up a creek.

There was only one person in town who probably could find her and would bother to give her a ride.

She scrolled through her contacts and found Sam's number.

Sam drove down the street slowly. God, was everyone at Walmart today?

He finally noticed her pacing behind a bench by the entrance. Sam honked the horn and she looked his direction.

Amelia stopped on the curb as he pulled up and then opened the door when he put the car in park.

"Thanks. And I'm sorry. You're the only person I now in this damn place."

"You're about fifteen miles from your hotel, did you know that?"

"Only fifteen? I need to get back to training harder."

This woman was a mystery.

Sam pulled out of the parking lot and headed toward the highway. "I take it this wasn't one of your planned runs."

She shook her head. "Not even close. More like a cool down run. A clear-your-mind run." She let out a snort of a laugh. "Oh, who the hell am I trying to kid? It was an *I'm pissed as hell* run."

Ah! So the wives weren't getting along. "Did something happen with Penelope and Vivian that I should know about?"

"Yeah, we all got screwed." She let out a loud breath and then turned in the seat so she was looking right at him.

"The son-of-a-lying-bitch was cheating on me."

Sam slid her a glance and then focused on the road. Of course he'd cheated on her. He had two other wives. The run must have made her delusional.

"Don't look at me like that," she said crossing her arms over her chest. "I know what you're thinking. It's very obvious he cheated on me. What I mean is he was picking up girls at bars and taking them home."

"How do you know this?"

"Because that's how he met Penelope. He picked up one of her friends the night before he moved in on her."

"And she knew that?"

Amelia nodded. "See, he had a way. Oh, God, did he have a way."

Sam's fingers tightened around the steering wheel. It shouldn't bother him that a married woman was in his car and he assumed she was going to talk about sex with her husband. But this particular woman had gotten under his skin. In two days they had spent an awful lot of time together.

"Let me get this straight. You're mad because your husband, who married you when he was already married and then married another woman while married to you, was having casual sex with other women?"

Her lips pursed and she turned back in her seat. "Yes. As irrational as it seems it pissed me off more."

Sam wanted to laugh, but this wasn't a laughing matter. There were real feelings being had and three very hurt women.

"I can't imagine you let anything get under your skin."

"I'm still a woman."

Ouch. He was fully aware that she was a woman and too much aware that he was attracted to every inch of her muscular frame—which could crush him for even having the thoughts. But there was something else that she wasn't letting go of. In two days he'd learned that she spoke what was on her mind and ran to get it off her mind. Something still gnawed at her.

Sam drove her back to the hotel and parked in the lot.

"Will you be alright?"

Amelia let out a heavy breath. "Yeah. No need to be angry anymore. It's only going to cause me to create holes in my shoes."

He snickered. "I'm here if you need me."

She nodded and opened the door. "I've never needed a man." That hurt, he thought. "But it seems like in the last few days I've learned to need you."

Sam felt his mouth drop open and that had made her smile.

"I'll see you tomorrow," she said shutting the door.

"Hey," he called though the window after her as she started toward the building. "You've been my dinner date for two nights. Interested again?"

Her shoulders dropped and she shook her head. "I think Penelope needs some company." She gave him a wave and disappeared into the building.

Sam sat there for a moment longer. Disappointment was an understatement of what he felt. And worse, after tomorrow Amelia Monroe would leave Parson's Gulch, Oklahoma and head—somewhere else.

He put the car into drive and pulled away from the building. She wouldn't be the first woman he'd wanted to get to know better—maybe she wouldn't be the last.

Chapter Five

It had been a long time since Amelia had been nervous. Usually she could compose herself with shoulders back and a tight jaw, but today was different.

She'd dressed in a long skirt and a beaded tank which she belted at the waist. Penelope had actually gasped when she'd seen her.

"You're stunning. No wonder Adam fell in love with you," she'd said as they'd maneuvered around each other in the small hotel room that morning.

If only she knew he'd probably only seen her like this a few times. It was the strong woman type that he said he'd liked about her. But obviously he had a flair for feminine too. Looking at Penelope with her blonde curls and her curves and thinking about Vivian and her sophistication, Amelia wondered what he saw in her at all.

Amelia parked her truck in front of the building where Sam's office was. This would be a different side to the man she'd been spending so much time with. He'd have to be official and boring, she figured. Then she thought about him with his sunglasses on in those running shorts which had made his ass look so good—she had to clear her throat to clear her mind. He'd been nice to know, but in the next hour their short lived friendship would be over and she'd drive away from Parson's Gulch for good.

She looked at Penelope who was gripping tightly to her purse. "Are you okay? You're not going to be sick are you?"

Penelope shook her head. "I'm just afraid that other woman is going to yell at me. I honestly didn't know about her or you. I just feel like I've done something so wrong."

"Just remember she's in the same boat. She's even more jilted than either of us. We just need to go in and hear what Sam has to say and then go our own ways."

She saw the threat of a tear in Penelope's eye.

"I'll be sorry to not have you around," she said as she lifted her head and looked at Amelia. "My baby is all I have. I just don't know the first thing about being a mother."

Amelia felt the tightening in her chest and she knew what it was. It was the offer to help take care of her lodged inside of her.

She smiled and then opened the door to the car. She'd see what happened in the next hour and then she could make up her mind on what she wanted to say to Penelope. After all, Amelia had nowhere to go either.

Sam's office was on the third floor and the elevator was out of order.

By the time they'd reached his office Penelope didn't look well at all.

"Listen, there's a restroom down the hall. Why don't you go and freshen up. Splash some water on your face and just get yourself pulled together. I'm going to go in and tell Sam we're here."

Penelope nodded and walked down the hall.

Amelia stood outside the door that read S. JACKSON ATTORNEY AT LAW and sucked in a deep breath. She was about to face Vivian Monroe for the first time really. This would be the first time she'd hear her voice and surely there would be some blame. Normally Amelia would handle her anger with some sort of physical violence, but she couldn't do that here. She needed composure. She was trained for that. Her mother was deeply embedded in her DNA.

There was a part of her that knew seeing Vivian wasn't what was making her so nervous—it was knowing this was the last time she'd see Sam.

With a shaking hand, Amelia twisted the knob on the door and let herself into the office.

She opened the door to the waiting room where a woman, who must have been in her seventies, sat behind a reception counter.

"Mrs. Monroe?" the woman asked and Amelia thought that the woman had an easy job this morning. Everyone who walked through the door would answer with a yes.

"Yes. I'm Amelia."

The woman smiled and stood from her seat. "Mr. Jackson asked to see you in his office."

Amelia plastered a smile on and followed the woman down the hall. They passed a board room where the door was only slightly open, but she saw the black dress and shiny high heels of a woman—Vivian Monroe.

The smile on her face began to hurt, but she kept it in place.

The woman tapped on the door and then opened it.

Sam was standing behind his desk in a gray suit with a red tie. He had on glasses, which he promptly took off, but it didn't stop her body heat from rising. God he was one sexy man.

"Thank you, Mom."

The woman smiled and shut the door. Amelia quickly turned to see the woman disappear as the door closed and then turned back to Sam.

"Mom?"

He nodded. "She's been at the firm longer than I have. My father started it before I was born."

"Oh." She clasped her hands in front of her and noticed that he took a long look at her from head to toe and back again.

"You look beautiful."

She could feel the heat in her cheeks and she wished she hadn't reacted to that. "Thank you."

He moved across the office toward her, not picking up the stack of papers on his desk. His eyes were locked on hers.

"I've been thinking. You said you really didn't have anywhere else to go back to. You thought you needed a new place to start over."

Amelia felt the plastered smile diminish as her mouth fell open. She blinked and then moistened her lips. "Right."

Sam stepped in closer. His cologne, though applied lightly, was heavy in her nose. He was so close that for the first time she noticed the small mole just at the top of his dimple—accentuating his smart and sexy smile.

He moved even closer, forcing her to take a step back which had her back flat against the office door. Her lips parted as she watched him move close enough, balancing his hand next to her head against the door.

"I'd like you to think about staying in Oklahoma." His voice had grown soft and warm.

She swallowed hard. "Why?"

The corner of his mouth lifted deepening the dimple. "I've had a lot of time to think about you the past few days and I'd like to get to know you better."

Her hands were pressed flat against the door now. She could have him on the floor broken into pieces in the matter of just a few seconds, but something told her this man would never be a threat—at least not physically.

"This isn't very professional is it?" she asked as he moved in even closer.

"Least professional thing I've ever done. I'm crossing at least a dozen lines of ethics just having you in here with the door closed."

She could feel his breath on her cheek now. "Do you do this with all the women you represent?"

"I've never done this to a woman ever." His hand came to her hip. "And to do it to one that could kill me right now has my heart beating just a little too fast."

She couldn't help it. She raised her hand to his chest to confirm his racing heart—he was right.

"Why now? Why me?"

"Can't help myself. I can't get you out of my head and I can't let you walk out of that meeting today and drive away like you're planning to do."

"So you're going to seduce me?" She let her eyes lift to meet his.

"Is it working?"

"Yes," she said as she finally took hold of his tie and pulled him to her.

Sam's breath stuck in his chest as his body was pulled against hers. The only balance he had was his hand still pressed against the door. The hand which he'd placed on her hip to entice Amelia now held tightly to her as her tongue passed through his lips.

She had hold of his tie and her other hand wound up into his hair. This wasn't how he'd planned this. He'd given a lot of consideration to the fact that he'd probably be in a fetal position on the floor having been kicked in the balls. They were aching, but not because she'd hurt him.

He could lose his license. This was so wrong—and so right.

The knock on the other side of the door had their bodies jar apart and he swallowed that air he'd been holding.

"Yes?"

"Mrs. Monroe and Mrs. Monroe are here and they are waiting for you and Mrs. Monroe." He could hear the humor in his mother's controlled voice.

"I'll be right there." He looked down at Amelia who was looking up at him with eyes still hazed over from emotion. "There is a bathroom right over there and it opens into the hallway. Go gather yourself up and I'll head across the hall." He stood back up slowly and adjusted his tie.

Amelia passed by him and walked to the bathroom.

"Hey," he called after her. "Are you driving away right after?"

Her cheeks were flushed and her lips were swollen pink. Someone was going to notice.

She didn't answer. She only gave him a sexy grin and shut the door.

Sam let out a long breath, closed his eyes, and sucked in another. With the back of his hand he wiped his lips, just in case she'd decided to wear lipstick with that getup she'd had on. He picked up the stack of papers and headed toward the door.

When he opened it he could hear the sound of a chair as if someone stood and pushed it against the wall. The hair on the back of his neck rose as he heard Vivian Monroe's voice rise over the blood which had been running through his ears.

"What do you mean you're Adam's wife too?"

He rolled his head from side to side to work the tension out of his neck.

AMELIA

He was so going to hell for all of this.

Chapter Six

When Sam walked into the conference room Penelope was standing across the table from Vivian in tears. Her hands visibly shook and her teeth were chattering.

And how had Amelia made it into the room faster than he had? He had only turned around to pick up his papers.

She looked more like herself now. She'd somehow managed to run through that bathroom and tie her hair up in a ponytail—though still looking damn sexy in that skirt she had on.

Vivian's eyes locked on his. "Is this some kind of joke? Are you kidding me? How many more bimbos are going to flood in here and say they are married to my husband?" Her voice was loud and sharp. He had a headache brewing.

"Mrs. Monroe, please have a seat. We will get this all sorted out."

He looked toward Amelia, who had her hands on Penelope's shoulders and was easing her into a chair. She handed her a glass of water and waited until she'd sipped it to sit down herself.

Sam was finding it hard to breathe though all of this.

He set his stack of papers on the table and pulled out his chair.

"First, I'd like to extend my condolences to you all. I know this isn't what any of you expected."

Vivian had crossed her arms over her chest and locked her jaw. Her manicure was chipped which said to him that she'd been nervous. That made her a bit more human in his book.

"Mrs. Vivian Monroe," he said thinking it would make it easier to address them. "This is Amelia and Penelope—Monroe."

Vivian looked them both over and then focused her eyes back to the table. This was his signal to get it over with.

Sam sorted through the pile of papers

"I don't understand this Mr. Jackson. Why are we all here?" Vivian's voice was low and she still looked down at the table. "I haven't heard of people having to go to a reading of a will in—forever. What is it that he didn't tell me besides the obvious?"

"Well, Mrs. Monroe, he changed his will before he left for Iraq."

That had Vivian Monroe's head snapping up. "Changed it? Why would he do that?"

Sam shifted a look toward the other two women at the table.

Vivian's nostrils flared as if she were holding back a rush of tears.

"Can he do that? Is that allowed?"

"Yes. It was his will." Sam took the copies of the will and dispersed them among the women. "He had me draft this up prior to his leaving for Iraq. He also gave me this envelope to read after his funeral." Sam swallowed hard. "Please know that he didn't sit down and tell me he'd married three women. He asked me to assemble you all if he should die, but until I did—I was unaware of your connection." Of course when he'd met him in Oklahoma City only a few months earlier he hadn't anticipated this day would come so quickly.

Already Vivian was tearing through the pages of the will. "Where are provisions for me and the kids? I'm not in here."

"Mrs. Monroe…"

"Don't Mrs. Monroe me. I have two growing children. I have a car payment. I have rent. All of these things have his name on it. All of these things I depend on have his name on it."

Sam nodded his head. "I understand."

He saw her eyes fill with tears and her lips purse tight. "It says he left everything to Amelia."

"What!?" Amelia picked up the copy of the will in front of her. "I don't want this."

"Good. You shouldn't have anything. How dare you move in on someone else's husband like that?"

"I did no such thing."

"I married him when I was twenty. I had years invested in that marriage. You ruined that." She was looking right at Amelia whose face was growing darker in color, shaded by anger.

"The moment I found out he was married I filed for divorce."

"Divorce? Your marriage wasn't even legal."

Sam held up a hand and the envelope he'd torn open as the women began their banter. "Um, I think we'd better settle down."

"I would like to say my piece," Amelia said directly to him. Her eyes were even darker than when he had kissed her and he knew this was her attack mode. Now he certainly wished he had more people in his office to help than just his mother.

Amelia rested her hands on the table with her palms down. "I didn't go out to steal *your* husband. I met a man and I fell in love. He asked me to marry him and I did. I never, and I mean never, would have thought that he had a family somewhere else."

Vivian's lips twitched. "What about you?" She nodded in Penelope's direction. "You seriously didn't know he was married too? You can't be over nineteen."

Penelope batted her eyes quickly as the tears had already begun to fall. "I'm twenty-one."

"Oh, that's so much better," Vivian said with her hands in the air.

"Leave her alone. She didn't know about any of this," Amelia warned.

Vivian turned back toward Sam. "Listen. I was married to him for ten years. I have his two children. I'm not asking for millions of dollars. I'm not looking to settle everything with what he may or may not have had. But it was his wish that I stay home and raise our children and I did that. He can't just go giving everything he has to someone else."

Sam took a piece of paper out of the envelope and slid it toward Vivian. She looked down as he did so and then back at him, her eyes open wide.

"Why did he give that to you? Why do you have it?"

"It was in this envelope," Sam clarified. "I haven't opened it until now."

Vivian sucked her lips in between her teeth and he could see her fight off the tears that would be there soon.

"He never signed our marriage license." The tears were now falling as she looked down at the paper. "We got married in the back yard just hours before he deployed for the very first time." She sucked in a breath. "He took the license, tucked it into the pocket of his uniform, and said he'd finish it up. He kissed me goodbye and he was gone for nearly a year."

Vivian wiped at her cheeks and Sam handed her the box of tissue at his side.

She gave him what he'd consider a grateful look and took one from the box.

The other two women sat there with their eyes open wide as Vivian had spoken. The entire room had realized because he'd never filed the paperwork Vivian Monroe had only changed her name. She wasn't legally married to Adam Monroe. Though Sam considered that common law.

"For the record you assumed you were married?"

Vivian looked up at him with pleading eyes. "Well, yes. He said we were. He promised me…" She looked toward the other women and there was an understanding in that moment.

When she'd wiped away more tears she looked back at Sam. "I can't afford to live without his paychecks. They didn't always come on time. He'd forget to give me money for the electric bill and I'd have to borrow. But it was something. Now what do I do?"

Sam reached his hand over and placed it atop of hers. "Let's finish through this and then we can decide what legal action we need to take."

Vivian nodded in agreement and placed her hands in her lap.

Sam was very familiar with the will. He'd looked it over many times after it had been drafted. But, he'd admit he thought perhaps when they'd penned it, generically, that Amelia Monroe was an elderly relative—not another wife—or the woman he'd someday literally sacrifice his career for.

"Amelia is the full beneficiary. She will assume ownership of Mr. Monroe's personal belongings, bank accounts, pension, and investments."

"Investments?" Vivian's hands flew in the air again. "He didn't have investments. I'm on his bank accounts. She can't have the ones my name is on."

Sam pulled more paper from the envelope. "It seems he had many accounts, Mrs. Monroe."

"She can have whatever they had together," Amelia said quickly. "This is all absurd anyway. Why me?"

"You were his only legal wife."

All eyes turned to Penelope whose mouth had opened with a tiny squeal.

"I'm sorry Mrs. Monroe. The man who performed your marriage was not licensed to do so. Your paperwork was not filed with the courts correctly either I'm afraid."

The room filled with a thick silence. There were three Mrs. Monroes, but only one legal one.

"Mr. Jackson," Amelia bit out and he didn't like the sound of his proper name on her lips. "What do I need to do to go about securing what was left to me?"

Vivian stood this time. "You're going to take it? What kind of woman are you? I have kids to feed."

"And your kids will be fed."

"You don't deserve this. You can't have this. I'm going to fight it."

"You can't afford to fight it," Amelia pointed out.

Vivian's eyebrows narrowed in. "He was *my* husband. Ten freaking years!" She slammed her fist to the table. "I'll find a way to fight you for what should be mine."

Amelia exchanged glances with Penelope and then looked back at Sam. "I need this. I need what he left me."

"I have all the papers here. The accounts and..."

"Bitch!" Vivian was walking around the table and that was when Sam and Amelia got to their feet.

Sam watched as Amelia held her hand out as if to just say stop—as if she were Darth Vader and had the force. And Vivian stopped.

"Listen," her voice shook, but only with a resonating anger which he knew was filling her body and not the fear of women getting out of control, which was filling his body. "I respect that you need to take care of your family. I'm not going to let anything happen to you. But Penelope was his wife too."

"Their marriage wasn't legal," Vivian pointed out and then it was evident by the look on her face that hers wasn't either.

"Penelope doesn't get cut out," Amelia said again firmly.

"And you? You're just going to take all of it? Give us a little crumb and run off?"

"I don't want anything the asshole had. He screwed up two years of my life and then messed around behind my back. I don't need his money or his crap."

"Then just sign it over. She'll be fine."

Amelia took a step toward Vivian and that prompted Sam to move in, though he wasn't sure what he'd do.

"I said you'd be taken care of and so will Penelope."

Vivian's face was contorting in her anger. "Why? Why does she deserve anything? My kids deserve it. They lost their father. Do you know what that does to a kid?"

"I lost my mother to a sniper in Desert Storm. I have a good idea."

He watched as Vivian stepped back and her face softened. "I'm sorry," she said softly.

She walked back around the table.

"I just don't understand. If you were trying to divorce him before he deployed and he was only gone six weeks," Vivian looked at Penelope. "You couldn't have been *married* long."

"Two months, ma'am."

"Two months?" Vivian's shoulders dropped. She looked back at Amelia. "Really? She's worth everything he had for a two month marriage? Ten years," she reiterated jabbing a finger into her own chest. "Two kids. Please, just do the decent thing and walk away."

"She deserves it as much as you do. She's going to need his help too."

"Why would she…" Vivian's eyes went wide. Sam was sure she'd quit breathing. He stood just as Vivian sat back down in her chair. "Son-of-a-bitch."

Amelia nodded. "Yeah."

Sam darted his eyes from one woman to another. He probably had more education than anyone in the room, but he was lost. He hated days where the estrogen in a room was much higher than the testosterone.

Amelia finally looked up at him and she must have realized he was lost.

"Penelope is expecting Adam's baby."

Chapter Seven

Things weren't much different for the next hour. Penelope cried and said, "I'm sorry," about six thousand times. Vivian fought for her rights, denounced Adam and cursed his name, cried, and fought again. She'd asked for a computer to look up the marriage information. She'd made phone calls. But to no avail. Adam had left her hanging— he'd never filed their marriage.

Sam watched and intervened when he needed to, but it seemed to him Amelia was running the show.

For being such a strong woman that any man in his right mind should fear, she was very soft and caring.

She saw to it that Penelope drank water and kept calm. At one point she'd moved to the other side of the table and sat next to Vivian and placed her arm around her shoulders. He was sure she'd asked about the children which at first had eased Vivian, but at some point she'd snapped and then told her that they were none of her business. Amelia had then moved back to Penelope as his mother brought in sandwiches and cookies.

Sam wasn't sure about that move. He'd hoped they'd all get so hungry they'd need to leave.

He looked at Amelia now holding Penelope as she sobbed and he thought he was hungry—for her.

Realizing that the battle ahead of him was just that—a battle—he wondered why he'd even approached Amelia in his office. But he just couldn't help himself. He'd never made a move on a woman like that in his life. Let alone a widow who had just—just—buried her husband.

The woman could physically break him in half and carry his body to the ocean and toss him in. Why was he doing that to himself?

When he looked up at her again she gave him a soft smile as she rested her cheek against Penelope's blonde curls. He was in trouble. If this woman took her inheritance and left him he certainly was going to suffer a broken heart.

Amelia was exhausted. Adam had certainly screwed them all over. What the hell did she need his crap for and what was all this about her marriage being the only one that was legal?

She gritted her teeth. The part she really was angry about was that from what Sam had presented to them—Adam was fully aware that their marriage was the only legal one.

Penelope sucked in a breath and Amelia sat back, leaving her hand on Penelope's back.

"I'm very tired," Penelope said softly as she wiped away tears. "What do we need to do? I mean, I don't understand why you needed me here. Obviously there was no need for me."

Sam clasped his hands and leaned his elbows on the table. "Adam had asked for you to be here. I'm sure that even though this seems like a mess Adam assumed you three would handle it."

Vivian scoffed. "He was a game player, obviously. He loved puzzles and riddles. This is crap though." She looked down at her watch. "We've been here nearly two hours. I have a sitter I'm paying. What more do we need? I obviously need to find a job, sell my car, and move."

"No," Amelia said firmly. "Ladies, this sucks. If he weren't dead I'd think about killing him over this. But, it is what it is and we have to deal with it. I hate that he left me anything, but I'm not going to forget you. You all have his children to think about."

Vivian gripped the pen she'd been holding and Amelia was sure soon enough that ink would be all over that pretty dress.

"Sam, can we meet again? I think I know how to make this all better, or at least manageable, but I think we all need a break."

Vivian looked up. "You want to just walk away with everything right?"

"I told you, I'd make sure you were taken care of. You can either trust me or lose everything. I think in your shoes I'd start to trust."

"Trust isn't what has the four of us sitting in a room together."

"Well, maybe we should learn from this," Amelia said as Sam stood.

"I'm fine with all of you coming back tomorrow. I'd like to see everything wrapped up as well."

Vivian had taken a breath and Amelia was sure it was to make some comment none of them wanted to hear. But she closed her mouth, stood, and hoisted her purse over her shoulder.

"What time tomorrow? I have to find a sitter again."

"And," Amelia interrupted, "I will make sure the sitter is financially covered as I'm the one asking to come back."

"Generous of you," Vivian said, but there was an underlying tone of sarcasm.

"Let's meet here again tomorrow at ten," Sam said.

"Fine." Vivian was the first to walk out of the office.

Amelia heard Sam's mother wish her a nice day, but there had been no reply.

Penelope hadn't stood. Instead she rested her head on her folded arms on the table.

Amelia rested her hand on her back. "Are you okay?"

"I'm exhausted. That took a lot out of me."

"C'mon. I'll drive you back to the room."

Sam stood and moved toward them. "I have a very nice couch in my office and a blanket. Why don't you rest there for just a few moments? I'd like to talk to Amelia if you don't mind."

Penelope raised her head and nodded.

Sam escorted her across the hall and returned a few minutes later, shutting the door to the room behind him.

"You're not going to seduce me again are you?" Amelia raised an eyebrow.

"Something tells me trying that more than once in one day would be dangerous. Besides it seems you're the only married woman around."

"Right." She crossed her arms over her chest. "Widowed—remember that."

He nodded and then sat back down where his paperwork was and she followed.

"I don't mean any disrespect, but why did he leave you everything when he had Vivian and the kids?"

Amelia shrugged. "I have no idea. We always did everything separate. Different accounts. Different credit cards. Hell, I leased the house."

Sam looked down at his papers. "I don't suppose anyone noticed that there really isn't much to what he left. In fact, by doing this he left a lot of different debts in his wake."

Amelia let out a breath. "I wondered about that." She leaned back in her chair and pulled the band from her hair. "We need to pay off those debts and take care of those kids."

"You could turn it all over. If you're okay financially and he didn't leave you with debt you could…"

"I promised Vivian her kids would be taken care of and they will be."

A smile formed on Sam's lips.

"What?"

He sat back in his chair. "You scared me the moment I met you. I didn't expect you to be this nice."

"I'm not nice."

"Yes you are. You don't want to be, but you are."

"I get my dedication from my mother. The nice and nurture come from my father."

"It's sexy."

"You're making a move on me again."

"I'll apologize in advance. I assume that'll keep happening until you tell me to stop."

She gave him a shrug. "I'll let you know."

That smile was back on his lips. What a prime opportunity to just dive across the table and yank that tie again, but she didn't. There were other issues at hand.

"We can't just divide up the money—or what there is of it. We need to clear his debts and take care of the kids. All three of them."

"Okay, what do you suggest if you don't divide it up?"

"See the money will run out. It'll go too quick. They both have expenses. Vivian has two mouths to feed and clothe. There's daycare and now she has to get a job. Penelope has nowhere to go. She has no job. No house. She's going to need prenatal care and eventually she'll have to pay for the delivery."

Sam laced his fingers behind his head. "You've given this a lot of thought."

"I think fast in what I consider crisis mode."

"And this is a crisis?"

"To them it is. I don't want any of this. I couldn't give a rip what he has. But he put me in charge for a reason."

"I assume he knew what he was doing."

"That'd be a first."

Sam stood and walked to the seat that Penelope had occupied. He reached across to his pile for a legal pad and a pen and then looked at her.

"Tell me what you're thinking."

~*~

At ten o'clock the next morning, Sam could hear his mother escort people into the room across the hall from his office. He hadn't had much sleep thinking about what Amelia had said to him. And it wasn't her plan that had kept him awake, it was the words *I guess tomorrow I'm going house hunting.*

He hadn't been able to think of anything else. She was staying in Parson's Gulch. She was going to embrace her Oklahoma roots. She was going to be near—him.

He hadn't made any more inappropriate moves and she hadn't done anything but tell him goodbye when she'd helped Penelope out of the office yesterday. But it was a good sign that she was staying.

Sam looked around his desk and began to gather up everything he needed when there came a tapping at his door.

He looked up expecting to see his mother, but instead there was Amelia smiling.

"I like you in glasses. You look very sophisticated."

Quickly he pulled them off his face. "They're kind of my nerdy secret."

Her lips pursed to conceal her smile.

She looked more comfortable today—more herself. Her hair was pulled back in a ponytail. She had on a pair of jeans and a beaded tank top, much like yesterday's, which showed off those amazing shoulders he'd love to rub.

Around her neck, she wore a necklace with something on it. He'd have to ask her about it.

"Heads up, Vivian needs to get out of here in an hour. She already has an employment interview."

He nodded. "I think I have everything put together so it shouldn't take long if they just go with the plan."

"I guess we'll see."

He stood and started for the door as she turned around and walked to the room. Sam slowed his pace. He was enjoying the view in front of him.

Penelope, who looked very tired, sat in the same place she had the day before. She wore a tank top and a pair of shorts that Sam was sure she wouldn't be wearing much longer. Vivian sat in the same seat she'd occupied the day before as well. She too had on a pair of jeans and a fitted T-shirt. Her hair was straight and hung over her shoulders. Today she sported glasses. It was then Sam realized she was much younger than he thought she was. He did some quick math to realize that if she'd married Adam when she was twenty and had been *married* for ten years she was only inching into her thirties.

"Good morning, ladies." Sam put on his professional smile and waited for them to return the gesture, but he wasn't going to get that. He was use to that. "Amelia Monroe, who as we established yesterday as the sole heir to Adam Monroe's assets, has proposed a plan to secure the assets for long term gain for you, Vivian, and you, Penelope, to ensure for the caring of your children."

Sam pulled out a packet for each of the women and handed it to them.

"Adam had incurred a substantial debt while away as well as having invested some of his savings. Mrs. Monroe would like to pay off the debts and then use the money left for capital toward a business venture."

"Nice. Leave him debt free and gamble his money." Vivian pushed aside the plan in front of her.

"Why don't you listen to the rest of the plan?" Amelia urged through gritted teeth.

Vivian narrowed her eyes at Amelia and Sam cleared his throat. "Amelia suggests that the three of you go into business together."

Vivian was on her feet. "Are you kidding me? I'm not going to go into business with two women who slept with my husband."

Sam could see the crust of Amelia's calm begin to crumble.

"Slept with your husband? This is what you think this was?" Amelia pushed herself to her feet keeping her hands planted on the table and Sam moved to the edge of his chair in case he needed to intervene—though if Amelia made a move, he knew he'd never get her off of Vivian.

Amelia focused her eyes on Vivian. "Listen sister, this wasn't some one night stand for either of us. I thought I'd married a soldier with decent morals. I was wrong. You were wrong. Only Penelope knew what kind of man he was and she still fell in love with him."

"What does that mean? *Kind of man*? She knew he was married?"

"No, she knew he was picking up women at bars."

Sam saw the flash in Vivian's eyes and then the retraction. "Oh."

"It never was just the three of us. We were the three he kept. This seems to have been a game to him."

Vivian lowered herself into her chair. "I never thought about that." Her shoulders dropped and Sam eased back into his seat as Amelia sat down in her chair as well. Vivian covered her mouth with her hand and then looked at Amelia. "How long were you married to Adam?"

"Two years."

Vivian batted her eyes fighting back tears which Sam could see forming. She swallowed hard. "When?"

"April—why?"

The first tears rolled and Vivian wiped them clean with the back of her hand. "Did you go on a honeymoon?"

"Quick trip to Florida."

Vivian nodded. "Lots of sun there."

"It was very warm. What does this have to do with any of this?"

Vivian blew out a breath. "When Emma was born four years ago, Adam was in Iraq. They did a live feed and he saw her be born."

"That's precious," Penelope finally spoke.

Vivian nodded. "When Ava was born, my sister was there with me. I hadn't been able to get a hold of Adam. I didn't even know where he'd been deployed—until now."

Sam saw the color leave Amelia's cheeks. "Florida?"

"When he came back two weeks later he had a really nice tan." There was a bite to her words.

"Oh, Vivian…" Amelia covered her mouth with her hand. "I didn't…"

"I know. You didn't know. I see that now."

Vivian's cheeks were red, but the tears had stopped. Anger had taken over and Sam wondered what had begun to brew in that head of hers.

"Would you ladies like to take a break?" he offered.

Vivian shook her head. "No. Just…no." She took a deep breath and let it out. Folding her hands on the table before her she lifted her head and looked at him.

"What does Amelia have in mind?"

Chapter Eight

Amelia reached into the bag which hung from her chair and pulled out a legal pad Sam had given her.

"I made a few notes. But I'm not the one making the decisions. First I think we should look into our backgrounds. What do each of us do?"

Penelope looked between Amelia and Vivian. "I've worked in coffee shops, clothing stores, a movie theater." She thought for a moment. "I've washed cars, sacked groceries," her eyes opened wide, "oh, and I worked at a day care center when I was seventeen. I only worked one summer, but I was really good with the kids."

Vivian shook her head as if she were disgusted by Penelope.

Amelia shifted in her seat and gave Vivian a glance. "What are your qualifications?"

Vivian's eyes went dark. "I have an associate's degree in early childhood development."

Amelia made some notes on the pad.

"What about you?" Vivian asked. "What skills do you have?"

"I could have broken Adam into a million pieces and no one would have known where I buried him."

She'd said it matter-of-fact, but it had brought out the strained smile Vivian had been hiding.

"It would be an interesting advertisement for any kind of business we put together," Vivian smirked.

"Might be big money."

This time Penelope laughed, then quickly covered her mouth with her hand.

Amelia looked at her very short list. "So the only thing we have in common is child care."

"The only thing Penelope and *I* have in common is child care. And children. You don't seem to fit into this picture."

Amelia nodded slowly. "I just own the accounts."

She watched as Vivian sat back in her seat crossing her arms over her chest.

Amelia looked at the list. One of Vivian's concerns was child care. That was a definite issue with her getting a job. And Penelope didn't know anyone so how could she get a job if she had to pay out for child care always?

But Amelia didn't know anything about children—nothing. She'd been one once, but that was as far as it went. But she did understand finances and business—enough.

Of course they could open a store with shirts and skirts and the kids could hang out. Maybe they could have a self-defense studio and she could teach them what to do.

"Are you going to let the rest of us in on your planning?" Vivian sat forward, her arms on the table.

"Sorry," Amelia said as she set the pen on the pad. "The common factor we have here are kids. Your two and Penelope's. No matter what we do or what jobs either of you take on you're going to have to find child care."

"Yeah, bosses aren't real fond of kids hanging around," Vivian snapped.

"No one is going to hire Penelope either." She looked to her side and saw that had brought a tear to Penelope's eye. "They don't want a pregnant woman who will leave and they will have to pay out medical benefits on."

"Where is this going?"

"My first thought is *we* go into child care."

Vivian let out a snort and sat back in her chair. "You're going to take care of children?"

"I was thinking I'd be the executive side. The two of you seem to have more knowledge about kids."

"Ya think?"

Amelia swallowed hard. If Vivian Monroe had crossed her path prior to Adam's funeral she was sure she'd have given that dark hair a firm yank that brought her to her knees. But as it was she was also the peace keeper, so she'd refrain from ripping Vivian Monroe to pieces.

"I'd love to work with kids," Penelope spoke softly. "I have four sisters and they were much younger than I was. I've done a lot of babysitting."

"This is more than babysitting," Vivian added.

"Oh, I know. But I like the thought that I could be with my baby too."

Vivian's eyes softened. "That is a plus."

Amelia watched Vivian process it. "It would mean thinking about it. A place, licenses, advertising. There is a lot to consider."

"It would take a while to get it all together. That's quite an undertaking," Penelope added.

"I agree. I could teach some martial arts and self-defense classes for a bit. That would help earn us some revenue."

"I could find a job for a few months. It's summer and the seasonal jobs which are filled by kids will need people to fill in," Penelope said as if she knew the facts behind that.

Vivian looked down at her hands clasped on the table. "I'll still need to find a job and have someone watch the kids."

Amelia pushed her shoulders back. "You have me and Penelope. We're a team now, even if we didn't plan that."

"You don't know my kids."

Amelia grinned. "I train soldiers. I can keep tabs on your two girls."

Vivian met her grin with one of her own. "You might be in for a lesson."

"I like a challenge."

Vivian actually laughed before she looked down at her watch. "I have to go." She reached for her purse and hiked it onto her shoulder. "So is this what we're doing?"

"Let's talk again. Give it some thought. Penelope and I need to find places to live. And we have to secure his debts too. I don't know what we'll have left. But without a plan..."

"We won't know where we're going," Vivian added.

"Right."

Vivian nodded. "Why don't you both come by my house tonight for dinner?" She stood. "I promise not to poison anyone."

Amelia laughed, but she noticed Penelope's eyes opened wide.

"I think that would be nice. I'll bring wine," Amelia offered and Vivian acknowledged with a nod before leaving the room.

Amelia sat back in her chair. "That went better than I thought it would."

"She doesn't have much choice," Penelope said softly. "She's broke, no job, two kids, debt. You're her saving grace. You're mine too."

Amelia's chest grew warm. She certainly hadn't planned on saving anyone but herself.

Penelope looked toward Sam who had been sitting quietly at the head of the table. "You don't by chance know of anyone who needs a temp? I can answer phones, file, email, fax—all that stuff."

Amelia tucked in her grin. Penelope was young, but she couldn't help but really like her.

Sam sat forward and rested his arms on the table. "Have you ever heard of Santa Rosa Beach, Florida?"

Penelope frowned and shook her head.

"There is a retirement community there. And in exactly three weeks my secretary will be returning there."

Her brows came together causing a crease in her forehead. "Your mother is your secretary, right? That's what Amelia said."

His eyes met Amelia's. "Yes. My regular secretary is on maternity leave."

"Imagine that," Amelia laughed.

"Something must be in the water," he added as he sat back in his chair. "She won't be back for another two months."

"You must have one helluva maternity plan," Amelia grinned, making sure he felt the heat from her eyes.

"She asked for a year off. We're almost through that year."

Penelope looked between them and then focused back on Sam. "So you need help? Mr. Jackson, I really can do the job."

Her curls bobbed as she spoke and her voice had gone down in pitch as she grew more serious.

Sam nodded. "Some of my clients can be...well..."

"Assholes? Oh, I can deal with that."

Sam laughed now. "Penelope, as long as you call me Sam when we're not with clients, I'd love to give you a chance."

Penelope stood from her seat and hurried to a very unprepared Sam. She wrapped her arms around his neck and hugged him tightly. "You don't know what this means!"

Amelia felt the moment tug at her and she wasn't used to feeling such joy for someone else.

Penelope backed away. "I should find an apartment. I have just enough saved for something little."

She bit down on her lip and her brows furrowed.

Amelia stood. "I can afford the room for a few more days. Just stay with me and we will find a place."

"Together?"

Amelia now had shocked herself. Was that what she'd meant? Would it matter? "We can think about that."

Penelope's eyes widened. "I think that would be fun." She turned toward Sam. "Can I go talk to your mother? Can I have her show me around?"

Sam chuckled. "Yes. That would be fine."

A squeal erupted from Penelope as she ran out of the board room and down the hall. Amelia shook her head.

"You didn't have to do that."

He shrugged. "I'll need someone anyway."

"And you think she will be the right person to fill that void?"

He leaned in. "Don't tell my mother this," he whispered. "But anything is better than my mother."

Amelia covered her mouth with her hand since it had dropped open. "I can't believe you said that."

Sam sat back in his seat. "Sometimes the truth hurts."

He stood and moved to the seat Penelope had vacated. With a gentle stroke he moved his hand down Amelia's hair. "I was going to ask you to dinner tonight."

"Seems like I have plans."

"So it does." He moved in closer. "The logical part of me says I should lie low for a while. I've already crossed so many lines of ethics…"

Amelia moved in closer yet. "I was hoping we'd get a chance to cross a few more of them."

Sam lifted his hand to her cheek and pulled her in. The moment his mouth moved against hers she knew she was walking a tightrope wire hung from the highest point, but she just didn't care. Adam had screwed her over and she'd long ago lost feeling for him. But Sam…well he was a wonder.

The moment was short and not fulfilling at all when the sound of a gasp was heard from the doorway.

They both looked up to see a very surprised Penelope.

Chapter Nine

Amelia sat in her dark motel room waiting for Penelope to walk through the door. She was counting on the fact that she had no money and nowhere to go, therefore she would return to the motel.

She'd spent the better part of an hour walking the streets near Sam's office looking for her. Sam had called a few friends in the area to keep an eye out for her, but she seemed to have vanished.

Amelia knew they'd been stupid to have done what they did. But damnit, she really liked Sam and Christ she really wanted to tumble with him more than once—but she'd just like to get to once.

Just as she thought it the door opened and a very tired Penelope walked through.

"I almost thought I was going to have to call the police." Amelia stood from the bed and moved toward her. "Where the hell did you go? Where have you been?"

Penelope looked up at her with swollen red eyes. "I've been walking."

"This whole time?"

Penelope shrugged. "Most of it. I headed back to Sam's office when I got tired. I didn't know where else to go. I sat in his office for an hour while his mother brought me snacks and he made me drink water."

"You went back to Sam's?" Her voice shook and that pissed her off. She'd been trained to have a solid voice. Having it shake wasn't an option.

Penelope nodded. "I'm not mad."

"You're not?"

"No. I'm sad."

All of this girlie emotion stuff wasn't resonating with Amelia. "You're sad that you saw me and Sam kiss?"

"Yes. I saved myself for someone who lied to me. Now I'm pregnant and he's dead—and a liar. And you have Sam."

"Sam and I aren't really anything. It just happened."

"He's nice."

"He is."

Penelope set her purse down on the small table and toed off her shoes. "Did you know him before? Before Adam died?"

"No. I only met him at the funeral before you walked in."

"Oh. He must really like you then."

"I'd like to think he does. Here, sit down on the bed. Put your feet up. You shouldn't have been walking that long."

Penelope moved past her to the bed, propped up the pillows and sat down as Amelia sat in a chair by the table.

"What do you think Vivian will say?"

Amelia's jaw tightened. "It's really none of her damn business," she sighed. "But I assume she'll accuse me of trying to gain something."

Penelope nodded. "That's what I thought too."

Where did they go from here? "I'll tell her if you want me to."

"What do you think?"

"There is part of me that says I should say to hell with it, leave town, and forget all of this."

Penelope's eyes grew wide with something that looked a lot like fear.

"I'm not going to," she assured her and Penelope's face softened a bit. "I like him and I should be able to screw who I want to since my own husband didn't care who he screwed."

Penelope rested her hands on her stomach and at the same time the reaction felt like a kick in Amelia's gut.

"I didn't mean that bad—Christ, it couldn't have come out good either."

"It's okay. I'm getting used to it. Vivian looks at me like I'm a disease. Her disease."

"You're not. You're as drug into this as we are. Even more so, you don't have anything to go on but his handsome face. Vivian can at least draw on some good memories for her girls."

Penelope wiped away a tear that had fallen from her eyes which had filled. "I should have decided not to keep the baby."

That had Amelia on her feet. "You wouldn't dare?"

"No. No." Penelope sat up. "I mean I should have decided a long time ago to make adoption arrangements. I don't know what I'm doing. I'm not mother material."

"Okay then." Amelia lowered herself back into her chair. "Sorry. Not my body. I shouldn't have gotten so upset."

"I understand. I can't lie—I thought of that too. But it didn't seem right. This baby," she put her hands back on her stomach and rested back, "is a gift. There is a reason that Adam left me this and it would be wrong of me not to give him—or her—a good life."

Amelia bit down on her lip. "I don't know anything about kids. Seriously—nothing. And as far as I'm concerned Adam was nothing but a conniving bastard. But still, I think there's hope for his kids—your baby. I won't leave you. I'll give you my word that I'm here for you though all of this."

Penelope's eyes shed more tears. "Really? You don't owe met that."

"No. But I like you and I don't have anywhere else to call home."

"What about Sam?"

Amelia scrubbed her hands over her face. "I don't know what do with that. I like him, but getting involved with him complicates things immensely."

"Vivian isn't going to like it."

Amelia sat back in her chair and pressed her fingers to her eyes. She knew Vivian would have a fit over it and she was more entangled with Vivian at the moment than she was with Sam. Perhaps it was time to let Sam go before it became something more.

~*~

Amelia pulled up in front of Vivian's house. It wasn't much, she thought. Adam could have done better for his wife and kids.

The driveway was crumbling. The wooden slats on the porch were broken and the shed door was off its hinges. This was just what she could see from the curb.

Penelope shifted her a glance. "Is this the right place?"

"This is the address."

"This isn't what I had in mind," Penelope turned and looked at the house again.

"Me either." She took in a long breath. "C'mon. Let's get this over with."

They climbed out of the car and Amelia reached back in for the bottle of wine she'd promised to bring.

There were toys on the porch and a hole in the screen door. Anger actually burned in Amelia's stomach as she reached for the broken doorbell button. How had he let them live like this while he was out picking up girls at bars. The thought made her sick.

Vivian opened the door, a dish towel in her hands. "Just in time. I just finished the garlic bread." She smiled at them and that too seemed odd.

Amelia and Penelope stepped through the door and into a whole different world filled with the scent of garlic and oregano.

The outside of the house surely didn't give any clue to what was on the inside.

The walls were brightly painted and the furniture was minimal, but set up so that the lines of the room looked bigger than they were and clean. There was a basket of toys in the corner of the front room, but no other signs that little girls might have played there.

They followed Vivian back to the kitchen, which was small, but organized in a very efficient way. The only table was in a small nook and there were flowers in a vase in the center and the table had been set for the three of them.

No doubt the kitchen had been updated a bit. Stainless steel appliances with a shine mixed in with dark cabinets and granite countertops.

"Your home is lovely," Penelope said as she looked around.

"The inside is," Vivian added as she stirred the sauce at the stove. "I now know he paid off his guilt in home renovations for me to keep quiet."

Amelia handed her the wine. "I hope you like red."

"It'll be perfect with dinner," Vivian said as she opened a drawer and pulled out a cork screw. "Penelope, can I offer you something? I have some juice, water, milk."

"Water would be nice."

Vivian pulled down three wine glasses from the cupboard and filled one with ice and water and the other two with wine.

She handed each of them a glass. "Here's to the son-of-a-bitch who has us all having dinner together."

They all tapped their glasses together, but Amelia wasn't sure if the toast was made for good health or in bitter anger.

"Where are your girls?" Amelia asked.

"Adam's parents took them for dinner." She shifted her eyes between the other two women. "I haven't told them anything yet."

Amelia sipped her wine. "I suppose they'll need to know. Especially since I was the beneficiary of the will."

Vivian took a long drink from her wine. "I'm just trying to decide how to tell them what an S.O.B. their son was. To them, Adam walked on water. To most of this town actually."

Vivian took another long sip and then set down the glass. "I think that's been the hardest part of all of this. I was married to Adam Monroe. Soldier. Star quarterback. Loving father," she said through gritted teeth. "His parents are upstanding citizens in the community and involved in the church." She picked up the wine and finished it off. "What will they all say when they all learn about the two of you?"

"I've never known a town to not have some kind of gossip. I guess we're it," Amelia said.

"Wonderful. And my girls?"

"We protect them," Penelope said softly.

Vivian's eyes narrowed on the overly optimistic Penelope. "Right. He'll rot in hell for what those girls will go through because of him." Vivian finished her glass of wine. "Let's eat."

90

She made a plate for each of them and they carried them to the small table.

"You're a good cook," Penelope said with her mouth full of spaghetti. "This is wonderful."

"This is simple. I didn't know how tonight was going to go."

"As long as you didn't lace this with anything, I'd say we're doing pretty good." Amelia took a large bite to prove that Vivian indeed didn't poison them.

Vivian set her fork down. Her face had gone serious and her eyes moist. "I don't know what to tell my girls. How can I ever explain who you are?"

Amelia swallowed her bite and then took a long sip of her wine. "I don't know. I can't see how you can't."

Vivian nodded. "I know. They're really small. I just can't say *Daddy had other wives…*" She looked at Penelope. "Other kids."

Penelope's eyes grew moist too. "Maybe you don't have to. We could just be friends of yours. I mean for all they know I'm having a cousin—well for now." She sucked in a breath. "But I'm having a brother or sister to them."

It was as if Penelope had only now realized the severity of the situation. Her baby was blood to Vivian's girls. They were a family—the children.

Penelope covered her mouth with her hands. "Oh, no. They're going to hate me. I've done such a bad…"

"Don't you go there," Amelia pointed a finger in her direction. "You didn't do this. He played us. So don't go taking blame for his shortcomings."

Vivian clasped her hands together and rested her head against them. "They're going to find out. In time they will see what he was. But I have to believe in the innocence of youth for now, right? They don't have to be told anything.

They are young enough. In time it will be—well it will just be."

"Maybe it would be easier if I just left. Disappeared," Penelope looked at both of them.

"How are you going to do that?" Amelia argued. "Sam gave you a good job. We'll find a place to live and we're going to create something for these kids."

Vivian looked at her. "Sam gave you a job?"

Penelope nodded. "His mother is going back to Florida. So until we start whatever we're going to start he took me on. For a few months at least."

"Generous."

Amelia picked up her wine. "The point is Adam threw us together. I can't imagine his plan was for us to stick together, but for the kids that's what we're going to do."

Vivian shook her head. "I still don't see why you stick around. You don't have kids."

Amelia sipped her wine and set the glass down. "I have nothing else to call mine either. I suppose it's as good a time as any time grow some roots."

Vivian filled her glass again from the bottle of wine. "So a daycare? Where the hell are we going to put that?"

"We will need to start small and expand from there. But, it just needs to gain enough revenue to keep each of us going. The prize is you both can be with your kids."

"And what do you get?" Vivian narrowed her eyes on her.

Amelia lifted her glass to her lips. "A fresh start."

Chapter Ten

Dinner hadn't sucked. Amelia was extremely surprised that they'd all made it out alive and Vivian hadn't tried to poison them.

She'd been rather surprised with Vivian's attitude the whole evening. They nearly got along like a group of old friends.

But things had changed when the girls came home and they all met Adam's parents. She'd kept a firm hand when his father shook hers and Penelope tried as hard as she could not to cry, but when she did on the ride back to the hotel, Amelia thought it was justified.

Neither of them had said a word to Adam's parents. Vivian would be the one to do that—in time. But first things first, they needed to keep planning.

They were all going to need jobs. Amelia and Penelope needed a home. And as Amelia rested her head on the pillow of her bed, she thought of Sam and there was a great need to see him because she was in need of some physical release—especially and after that play he made at her in his office. She grinned in the dark and figured he could use some physical release too.

The next morning Penelope was up and ready bright and early. Amelia figured she'd made as much noise as she could so it would wake her.

"I'm sorry. I didn't mean to wake you," she said as Amelia pulled the pillow over her head.

"Are you sure?"

"I need to get to Sam's. Can you give me directions? I know I watched when you drove there yesterday, but…"

"I'll draw them out."

She pried her head from the pillow and crawled out of the less than comfortable bed. Reaching for the pad on the nightstand, she wrote down the directions to his office.

"Thanks," Penelope said as she took the note. "Okay, well I'm off to work."

Amelia nodded. "I paid for the room for two more days. I'll have to head back to Georgia when we find a place and get my stuff. What about you? Do you need me to help you arrange that?"

Penelope bit down on her lip and shook her head. "I have everything."

Amelia narrowed her eyes on her. "Everything?"

"All I had in the world was myself and Adam. And I didn't have anything but a few shirts of his. And the baby." She rested her hands over her stomach. "I'm all ready to start over too."

She watched as Penelope gathered her things and opened the door. "Will you be coming by the office?"

"Why?"

"Well you and Sam. I don't know…to see him."

"I don't know if that's a good idea. A fling with Sam won't win over Vivian."

Penelope coughed out a laugh. "If she had sex with a man maybe she'd loosen up too."

Amelia shook her head. "I'm not sleeping with him," she said firmly, but Penelope only smiled.

"Not yet. I'll see you later."

When the door closed Amelia fell back in her bed. Crap—a man and two women was not the relationship status she was looking for. If he wasn't dead she'd kill Adam for this.

She let out a long breath. She might as well get up and decide how she'd handle the day. No matter what, she'd need to make a plan to move her stuff from Georgia to

Oklahoma. And since she didn't have any money, it looked like she'd be doing it on her own.

An hour later she was showered and dressed. A quick trip over to the coffee shop across the street—and something sweet—she'd start making plans.

However, once she got there and sat down, she'd spent two hours on her iPad, three cups of coffee, and because she couldn't help herself, two chocolate pastries. Moving to Oklahoma was going to make her fat. At the top of the To Do list she was making, she wrote in bold letters RUN.

She gathered her trash and stashed her iPad in her bag as her cell phone buzzed. She looked at it and smiled.

Mom is taking her apprentice to lunch. Would you be interested in meeting me for lunch?

She smiled when another text came through.

This is Sam.

The two pastries were still heavy in her stomach. Lunch certainly wasn't on her mind yet. But he was.

I'll meet you at your office.

She walked toward the corner and pushed the walk button. As she waited for the for the signal she looked at her phone and on a laugh she texted, *This is Amelia.*

~*~

Sam sat at his desk with his phone pressed to his ear, his glasses low on his nose, and a headache brewing behind his eyes. Constance MacMillan was giving him an earful about the tenant she wanted thrown out of the apartment she owned.

He was making notes on the pad in front of him, though he was actually doodling hearts and stick figures. It was official—he was pathetic.

"Okay, Mrs. MacMillan, I need you to email me all the specifics. I can't write it up if we don't have all the specifics as to why you want to evict him."

The conversation seemed to be starting all over again when Sam leaned back in his chair and noticed the woman in his doorway.

"Mrs. MacMillan, my next appointment just arrived. I'll wait for you to send that over."

Sam pulled his glasses off his nose and set them on his desk as Amelia stepped into his office.

"Did you dress up to see me?" he asked as he walked toward her.

"This is as fancy as it gets," she said looking down at her long skirt.

He loved the way her shoulders looked in sleeveless shirts.

"Anything special you'd like for lunch?"

Her lips parted and she licked them. He wondered if she wanted the same thing for lunch he wanted. They were certainly going to have to discuss that if this went any further between them.

She walked closer to him and reached for his tie. Sam swallowed hard.

"I'm not sure we have enough time for what I want for lunch. So I'll go wherever you have in mind." She nipped his lips with a small kiss and the heat under his collar rose.

"Suddenly I'm at a loss for suggestions." He let out a weak chuckle. He ran his hands down those muscular, soft arms he'd admired. "Would it be pushy to ask you to dinner before I even take you to lunch?"

She smiled slowly and batted those thick lashes over her dark eyes. "I was hoping you might."

He was trying to clear his head and think about lunch, but now that was nearly impossible. A chime rang out in the office and Amelia stepped back from him.

"Someone just came in. Have a seat. I'll be right back."

Sam walked around her and down the hallway. Vivian stood there with a daughter gripping each hand.

"Is everything alright?" Sam moved to her.

Her eyes were red, which he assumed was from tears since mascara was streaked down her cheeks.

"I need to talk to you."

"Of course."

At that moment Penelope and his mother walked through the door. He could see Vivian try to hide her face by bowing her head.

"Mom, would you mind if Mrs. Monroe's daughters sit with you? Maybe you could print out some coloring sheets for them."

"Of course," his mother said happily. "Do you girls like Disney princesses?"

They both nodded and went to his mother as he thought they might. He'd never seen a child who hadn't taken right to her.

He reached for Vivian's arm. "Let's sit down in the conference room. Can I get you something to drink?"

She shook her head and sat down in the same chair she'd occupied the two days earlier. "I'm sorry to barge in here like this."

"It's okay," he said pulling out a chair and sitting down. "What can I do for you?"

She reached into her purse and took out a stack of envelopes. "Adam's mother dropped these by today. They're bills. Lots of bills."

Sam looked at them. "There are car loans, credit cards, and phone bills here."

"Yes. All of this was forwarded to his parents' house." She sucked in a breath and batted back more tears. "They brought them to me so I could pay them off. They thought I was getting everything—you know. Everything he left to Amelia."

Sam nodded. "What did you tell them?"

Now the tears were back and streamed down her cheeks. "I told her. I had to tell her."

Vivian sobbed and her breath was in short pants. Sam wasn't so sure she wouldn't pass out.

"Take a deep breath," he instructed her as he set a hand on her back hoping to calm her.

Vivian did as he'd told her. When she'd composed herself she looked at him. "Perhaps I could get a glass of water."

He nodded and walked to the small refrigerator in the corner. He retrieved a bottle of water and handed it to her before sitting back down.

She opened it, sipped, and let out another long breath.

"I told her I wasn't his only wife. I told her Adam had married multiple times and he even had another baby on the way." Her lips pursed and Sam could see she was fighting back another wave of tears. "She said I was lying. She asked if the women she'd met last night were his *other wives*," she defined with her fingers making quotation marks in the air. "When I said yes she said they were gold diggers and they were lying. Her son wouldn't do something like this."

Sam rested his hand on hers. "It's expected."

"Maybe, but I don't know what to do. I don't think he has enough to cover all of this."

Sam looked over the extensive stack of bills.

"He had a life insurance policy and it'll pay off the bills."

"But there won't be anything left will there?"

Sam quickly did numbers in his head. The man must have felt his impending doom coming. Most of the credit card charges were within the past six months and the car loan hadn't had much paid on it. And where was the car? Adam Monroe seemed to have been collecting wives and then spending every loaned dime he could get his hands on.

"Listen, Amelia and Penelope aren't going to abandon you and your plans. We'll figure this all out."

"But his parents. I'm afraid they'll…well what if they sue me?"

"Sue you for what?"

"I don't know. They think I'm extorting him."

Sam shook his head. "He has nothing. And you have less."

She was batting at tears again. "His mother always thought I was using him. Don't get me wrong. She's been pleasant for the past ten years and she's always helped me out with the kids, but she's guarded against me."

"Why do you think that is?"

A smirk formed on her mouth. "My mother always said it was because I was too smart for her son."

"Maybe she was right."

"If I was so smart I'd have known he was messing around." The smirk and any hint of humor was gone from her face and her tone. "If I were so smart I'd have had a job before now."

"Vivian, you have heart. You trusted. You'll trust again."

"No. I don't want to do this again."

Sam wasn't so sure, but there was no need to discuss that now.

"Okay, well the next thing we need to do is tell Amelia and Penelope about this. They need to know that Mr. and

Mrs. Monroe know. This town isn't that big. There is a huge chance they'll cross paths someday. They need to be prepared."

Vivian nodded. "I'm not worried about Amelia. I'm sure she can handle them. But Penelope—I worry about her. I don't want her to be hurt."

Sam felt a warmth rush through him. From what he'd seen the past few days he wasn't sure there was much heart in the woman who had first been jilted by Adam Monroe, but he was wrong.

"I think the three of you will do just fine. No one will mess with you."

Finally, she smiled. "I guess I should call them. They need to know."

Sam bit down on his lip. "Penelope is here and I don't think Amelia is far. Can you sit for a few minutes?"

Vivian nodded.

"I'll have them come in."

Sam walked out to the waiting area and asked Penelope to go sit with Vivian in the conference room. "Have you seen Amelia?"

Penelope gave him a grin. "She ran to the corner to get a coffee. She didn't want Vivian to see her here."

Sam nodded. She was smart like that. He looked at his mother. "Send her back when you see her."

Fifteen minutes later Amelia walked into the room where they had the bills laid out on the table.

"I brought you a coffee," she said to Sam and he took the cup she handed him.

"Thank you."

"What is all of this?"

Sam and Vivian explained the meeting with his parents and the bills which had amassed.

Amelia sat in the chair next to Sam. "Can his parents do anything? Can they come after me?"

"They could fight his will. But then they'll be liable for all of this." He acknowledged the stacks of paper.

Amelia looked toward Vivian. "What kind of people are the Monroes?"

Vivian shrugged. "They're nice enough." She rubbed her palms together. "His dad is ex-military. So he was always strict and very blunt. His mother, well," she let out a sigh. "You know, I don't have to keep this in anymore. She's a bitch."

Her lips twitched and then she let out a laugh which she covered with her hands.

"I'm so sorry." Vivian tried to be more serious. "She's a wonderful grandmother and..." She tried to control another laugh that broke through. "But I have never liked her. I doted on her for Adam's sake. I have her watch the girls because they need their grandmother around. But she's always been snide to me. There's always been a comment here, a comment there. It was sort of refreshing to tell her that her son was a lying cheat."

Sam noticed Penelope tucking in her smile.

Vivian looked at Penelope and her laugh ceased. "Penelope, that wasn't fair. I'm sorry. She's the grandmother to your baby. I should have thought before I spoke."

"That's okay. I never expected that anyone would accept my baby once Adam died and I found out about the two of you. So I'd never considered her at all."

Amelia set her hand on Penelope's. "What about you? What family do you have?"

Penelope shrugged. "Oh I have a mother. But she does her own thing. I haven't told her where I am. In fact, I haven't talked to her in months. She doesn't know I got married. I was afraid if she saw Adam she'd, well," she looked away and then back at Amelia. "She's kind of a cougar. You know, an older woman who likes younger men?"

Amelia nodded.

"I was afraid she'd try to steal him from me."

Sam couldn't even imagine something like that. But he supposed it existed.

"I should hear from the insurance company here in the next day or so. We'll get these bills taken care of. But, without anything from Adam, what will you three do?"

Amelia looked at the other women. "We start our business. We're a team, right?"

He watched as the eyes of Vivian and Penelope both widened and lit up. Amelia Monroe might have just saved them all with that unselfish act. She could simply walk away now. There was nothing holding her there but a pile of debt. But she was willing to keep the bond they'd made in three short days and go with it.

Sam rubbed his damp palms on the legs of his pants. It was very possible he just fell in love with Amelia Monroe.

Chapter Eleven

Sam had missed out on his lunch date with Amelia. As his stomach grumbled he realized that meant he hadn't eaten either.

The thought humored him.

But he was on his way to pick her up for dinner and he didn't really have any intentions of taking her back to her hotel after.

He'd toyed with the idea of picking up a bouquet of flowers, but that seemed cheesy. It had been a very long time since he'd been this giddy over picking a woman up for a date, but this woman was different.

Who'd have thought a man like him would have eyes for a strong minded, and bodied, woman like Amelia? After all, Sam Jackson was—and he knew it—a wimp, a nerd, a full out Comicon geek.

And yet Amelia Monroe had pulled him in and kissed him when he'd tried to seduce her. She'd been hinting at more than just lunch today when he'd been hinting at the same.

Now, here he was parking his truck outside her hotel room and sex was a definite possibility. Less than a week—he'd known her less than a week. And even in the moment where he was thinking he'd finally broken the nerd status and he was some kind of freaking hero—he realized it was more than one night. He might have only met the woman and he hadn't had to woo her or anything out of the ordinary to turn her head. But still, Sam Jackson was a one woman kind of man. He wanted to keep her. He wanted her to stay in Parson's Gulch. He wanted it to be more.

The heat was rising under the collar of his shirt. Would she ever feel that way about him? Could she?

This was a woman who married a man like Adam Monroe. A woman who had openly admitted that after she'd kicked his ass she took him straight to bed.

Now his palms were sweaty again.

The door to her room opened and she stepped out. "Oh, hey. I didn't know you were here."

He nodded toward the two shopping bags she had in her hands. "Going somewhere?"

"To my car. I'm trying to pack up some of the stuff I've got. I have the room for one more night."

"Then what?" he asked, taking one of the bags from her.

"Then Penelope and I are homeless." She chuckled.

"I have room if you…"

"No." Her answer was quick and solid. "We'll get there in time." She unlocked the back of the Bronco and pulled down the tailgate. Sliding one bag in and then taking the other from Sam she smiled easily at him. "You would let me move in, wouldn't you?"

"I seem to have a soft spot for you."

She licked her lips and turned to him. "I've had you pressed up against me. There are no soft spots on you."

For the first time in his life he was praising yoga— quietly.

She pushed up the tailgate and rested her back against her truck. Reaching for his hands she interlocked their fingers. "If we're going to see each other I suppose I'll need to tell Vivian."

"Do you think she'll take it okay?"

"No." She smiled. "And I don't plan on telling her right away." She narrowed her eyes on him. "We are seeing each other, right?"

"I sure want to."

"Not just sex?"

He swallowed hard. "No."

"I would have taken you just for sex too if that was your answer." She gave his hands a yank that had him nearly plowing into her. "I really like you, Sam Jackson."

"Thank God."

He pressed his mouth to hers and she deepened the kiss from there.

When she pulled back, she said, "Where are you taking me for dinner? I can't stay out too long."

Sam dropped his shoulder and stepped back. "Do you have plans?"

Amelia's face grew serious. "Penelope. She's afraid to be alone."

"Why?"

"I think Vivian scared her talking about her mother-in-law."

He cringed. "We could take her with us."

Amelia raised her eyebrows and for a moment he thought she was going to accept that offer.

With a shake of her head she said, "She'll be okay until we get back."

With their fingers still entwined, she held his hand and walked back to the hotel. "I'm leaving tomorrow. Penelope is going to stay with Vivian until I get back."

"Where are you going?"

"I have to settle my life in Georgia," she said, slowing as they reached the door.

"Oh." His voice dripped the disappointment he felt. "How long will you be gone?"

"I should be back by Sunday."

Four days. Already he'd done the math and knew she'd be away from him for four days. Oh, he was pathetic.

"Anything I can do for you while you're gone?"

"Find me somewhere to live," she said pushing open the door to the room.

Sam's mind was already thinking of possibilities.

The air was thick and hot, but Amelia let her hair blow free with the window down. Sam had taken her to Oklahoma City for dinner, a bit of a drive, but secluded. There wasn't a part of her that didn't want to stay the night with him. But there was time for that. She could be patient.

"What kind of living arrangements are you looking for?" Sam asked when she'd gone silent for too long.

She turned toward him. "Something that has enough space for both of us." She thought again. "I guess something that has place for three of us. There are going to be three soon."

It was as if the air had grown even thicker.

"Penelope's baby." She pulled out her phone and made a note for Monday. "Do you know of a good OBGYN?"

Sam coughed. "Me? No. I don't have one in my contact list."

Amelia ran her hand over her face. "Sorry. I just realized she needs care. I don't think she's seen a doctor yet."

"We'll find her one."

"Crap. I need to find a job. She can't afford all of this on her own."

Sam reached for her hand and gave it a squeeze. "We can do that too."

Amelia pressed her head against the back of the seat. "That's the kind of guy you are, isn't it? You're not the kind that lets people just do what they have to do. You're the kind that steps in and makes things work."

He slid her a look and then turned back to the road. "Is there a problem with that?"

"Yes there's a problem." Her voice was rising over the sound of the air coming into the truck and the highway under their tires. "You just gave Penelope a job. You let Vivian come in and sob to you when all you had to do was read the will and contact the insurance people. I ask you if you know of a place to live and you're thinking about what I need. You'll find her a doctor and me a job. Who the hell are you? The Pope?"

"It seems to me you asked me for my opinion on most of those. Would you rather me not give it to you?" Now his voice had an edge. She was used to that. She brought that out in people.

"I just don't see where any of this is your problem."

"We're involved—remember? That's when it became my problem."

"And if Vivian or Adam's parents find out we're *involved* then you stand to lose a lot don't you."

Sam took the next exit and pulled off on the side of the road. He turned to her. "You're picking a fight with me. Are you more comfortable now? I may not be trained to kick the crap out of people but I do have a degree in argument. So what's it going to be? Are you going to let me help you with all of this or are you going to let me take my fee and walk away?"

Men she'd fought with over the years didn't use their words precisely to argue. They broke things. They broke people. This man would use his words and now she was out of her element.

"I'm sorry," she found herself saying for nearly the first time in her life. "I'm on edge. I have to close my life out in Georgia. I have to rethink all the plans I made when I asked Adam for a divorce. And then there's the baby."

She saw his eyes go wide as though a thought just lodged itself in his head. "Penelope's baby."

Sam nodded.

"The more I realize that baby is on the way the more I feel the pain in my gut from what he did. He used us. He cheated on us. He…he…it's so Goddamned unfair."

There was the slightest grin on Sam's lips. "Okay. This sounds more reasonable now."

He turned back to the steering wheel and put the truck in drive. When they were back on the highway he reached for her hand.

"I have a friend who has a townhouse in the center of town. He bought it a few years back when they put in the new development. Anyway, he rents it out for corporate use."

"Someone has their corporate headquarters in Parson's Gulch?"

He laughed. "No, but this certain company is based in Oklahoma City. They fly in CEOs and CFOs all the time who are here for a few months and then go on. Anyway, I could see if it's open and you two could stay there for a bit."

Amelia smiled. "That sounds nicer than some rundown apartment."

"It'll give you both some space. I'll call him tomorrow."

Amelia let out a sigh and turned to look at him in the glow of the sunset. "Thank you. You could have dropped me off on the side of the road back there, but you didn't."

"I might someday. Tonight wasn't the time."

That made her laugh. Oh, she liked him. Perhaps just a little too much.

Amelia drove away from Parson's Gulch, Oklahoma for the first time in a week. The sun was just coming up. It was beautiful to watch.

AMELIA

She'd made a few phone calls yesterday to people she knew in Atlanta. Her small condo had furniture that would need to be moved. She needed to close out some accounts. Quit her job. And she needed to rent a trailer because that car loan belonged to the Mustang in the driveway.

As she drove back toward the life she had, she plugged in her iPod and cranked up some Blake Shelton. Maybe some *Doin' What She Likes* would keep her mind focused on the task at hand—getting back to Sam.

Chapter Twelve

Because she couldn't turn off her head, Amelia had stayed the night in Memphis. She ate at an all-night diner and drove by Graceland just because it was there.

She'd finally driven up in front of the condo she'd once called home with Adam around ten o'clock Friday morning.

Home. She let out a snort. What a joke.

Seated on the front step of the building was Carson. She hadn't been sure about calling him to help her move, but he'd shown up. For that she'd give him the benefit of the doubt—and she'd press him for information.

Amelia parked her truck and turned off the engine. Before she could even climb out, Carson was hurrying toward her to open her door.

"Nice to see you, ma'am."

Soldier. At least he had manners and some discipline. "Nice to see you, Private."

"You can call me Carson, ma'am."

"And you can call me Amelia. I'm not married to your superior anymore."

The man rubbed his hands against his pants. "Right. I'm very sorry about your loss. He was a fine man."

Amelia bit the inside of her cheek. He was a fine soldier. He was a lousy man.

"Thank you for coming by. I need to get this all settled and move on."

"No problem. You mentioned you might need to sell some things too. I just got my own place. Maybe we could make a few deals."

"I think that would be just fine. Let's go inside and we can talk there."

Carson followed her up the steps and into her condo. It felt closed up—dark—dank. She went right to the patio door, retracted the blinds, and opened the door.

"I guess I left in a hurry," she said looking around. It wasn't like her to leave breakfast dishes on the counter or laundry on the table to fold, but she had. In hind sight she really hadn't had much time to think at all.

"What can I help you with first?" Carson asked.

Amelia smiled. "Well considering I didn't know I'd be moving, I didn't get any boxes."

"I can go down to the grocery store and get some." He tucked his hands into his front pockets. "Have you eaten anything? I could grab a pizza and some beer."

Amelia let her shoulders drop. "That would be great. I'll get you some money."

"No," he said quickly. "My treat."

With that he was out the door and she was alone in her own home—but it didn't feel like home anymore.

She looked around. Most of Adam had been removed before he'd deployed, after she'd found out he was married. But on the mantel was one picture. It was taken on the beach in Florida. Her chest pained and she rubbed between her breasts to make the pain she felt there go away. She now knew that while she was celebrating a new life wrapped in the arms of her husband, his wife was home giving birth to a baby girl.

Her stomach rolled and for a moment she thought she'd be sick.

Amelia reached up and lowered the frame so it was facing down. She didn't want to think about him anymore—but that wasn't going to happen.

She began cleaning out her belongings and putting her clothes into suitcases. She sorted out Adam's clothes. There wasn't much there. Before she left, she'd arrange to have a charity come pick them up.

Carson had returned with boxes and a pizza, which Amelia ate four pieces of and they each had a beer.

"Guess I was hungry," she said as she finished the crust of the last bite.

"Mourning can do that, ma'am."

So could anger, she thought.

She and Carson packed away everything into the boxes he'd brought. By the door were four bags of *items* to donate, which had belonged to Adam, as well as three bags of trash.

"What pieces of furniture did you want to discuss buying for your place?"

"Anything, ma'am. I don't have much at all."

She nodded and looked around. She hadn't had much either. A bed. A dresser. The couch, chair and coffee table, and the small two-person kitchen table. It wasn't until that moment she realized how minimal her life had been. Her thoughts went to Vivian's house—the inside of the house. The personal effects. Pictures of her children. Flowers in a vase. There was nothing personal here at all and never had been.

"I'll make you a solid deal," she said tying off another trash bag. "You showed up here under no pretense to help a widow clear out her things. The only connection we have was Adam. But you're a kind hearted man. I can tell that."

"Sergeant Monroe was a great man, ma'am. It's an honor to do this."

She swallowed hard. There was no need to burst the man's thoughts of someone he seemed to care for. "Well, I appreciate it. And I'll tell you what. You help me tomorrow load up the car and the boxes and all the furniture is yours."

His eye widened. "Ma'am?"

"I'm serious. I'm moving in…" she stopped and took a breath. "With some friends. I don't need all of this."

"Ma'am, thank you, Ma'am."

She smiled. "Come back in the morning. Around ten. We'll load up."

He nodded, thanked her and hurried out the door.

Now all she had to do was get a trailer.

A few phone calls and she was headed to a rental place to pick up a car hauler. Without the furniture all she had were suitcases and boxes. She and Carson could fill her truck and the Mustang with everything to get her moved. That might cut costs a little. She wouldn't need an enclosed trailer.

Once she'd driven away with the empty trailer she closed her accounts at the bank and headed to the martial arts school where she'd taught self-defense for years. The owner was certainly sad to see her go, but not surprised.

"Parson's Gulch? I've never even heard of it."

"It's a speck on a map, but just outside Oklahoma City. So really, it's not so small. There's a Walmart."

He laughed. "Well then, you're set." In a very gentle move he rested his hand on hers. "I'm sorry about your husband. He was a fine man."

She thanked him and left. If one more person told her how fine he was she might break someone's nose. It was time to get out of Atlanta.

That night she sat in her quiet, empty, boxed-up condo and just stared at the picture of her and Adam on their honeymoon. In his eyes there wasn't even the hint that something was amiss. How could he have just dismissed his family like that?

Her cell phone buzzed next to her and she looked at the screen.

AMELIA

I have no idea what to have for dinner. All my meals lately have been with you.

She laughed at Sam's humor.

Sam. She rested her head back on the couch. What an interesting man. Smart. Sexy. Interested.

She set the picture of her and Adam on the coffee table and picked up her phone.

I hadn't thought of dinner until right now. I guess I'm having left over pizza, she replied.

Then the phone rang in her hand.

"I think I'll have leftover pizza too," Sam's sexy voice breezed through the phone. "I figured I'd call and we could have it together."

"I'd like that."

She walked to the kitchen and opened the refrigerator. There was one slice of pizza left. It was a good thing she wasn't really too hungry.

"So how are things going?" Sam asked obviously with his mouth full.

Amelia pulled a piece of pepperoni off of her slice and popped it into her mouth.

"I gave away all the furniture. Boxed up all my things. Threw away all of Adam's. Closed out my accounts and quit my job. I guess you could say it's been productive."

"You did all that today?"

"I had some help from a young private who thinks the world of Adam."

She could hear the low hum from Sam. "Did you sock him in the gut?"

She laughed. "I thought about it."

She took a bite of the cold pizza, set it on the counter, and then went back to the refrigerator for a beer.

"This isn't home," she said softly as she leaned against the counter and opened the bottle. "This never was home."

"Do you think you'll find that here?" His voice broke and she smiled.

"Oddly enough I feel more at home there than anywhere. Even with his two other wives."

"Don't forget your in-laws."

She choked out a laugh. "Never even considered them."

"Well you might want to. They've asked for a meeting."

She pulled from her beer and swallowed it down slow. "Why?"

"They're a little confused."

"They haven't been giving Vivian a hard time have they?" She stood up straight. "They haven't gone after Penelope have they?" Her tone had risen in defense of the younger blonde she'd befriended.

"No." His voice was soft and she relaxed back against the counter. "Adam's father contacted me, after Vivian gave him my information. He says his wife is very out of sorts after Adam's death and he doesn't want her going after Vivian and tearing into her."

"Doesn't sound like a very good relationship."

"With Adam's mother and Vivian or between his parents?"

"Either."

Sam chuckled. "I get that too."

"So Monday?"

"Yeah, Monday. Around ten."

She thought about it. Perhaps she'd better get a job in Sam's office too. She sure was spending a lot of time there.

She heard her text message chime in her ear. Pulling the phone back she laughed.

"You're texting me while I'm talking to you?"

"I sent you my address. We have dinner plans on Sunday. I didn't want you to forget."

116

Amelia closed her eyes and breathed in the moment. "I couldn't forget."

"Just come by when you get into town. Oh, and I talked to my friend about the townhouse. It'll be up for rent in two weeks."

She let out a low hum.

"Vivian and Penelope are doing okay. Or did for one night. I can help you get a hotel room for a few weeks. You could sleep in my office. Or you could..."

"I'll work it out," she cut him off. She wasn't going to let him offer up her moving in again. Seeing each other was one thing. Knowing she was sure as hell going to be sleeping with him Sunday night—or she'd lose her mind— was another. Moving in with him was a mistake. She was tired of making mistakes.

"Okay, then," he said, but she could hear the hurt in his voice.

"Carson and I will have everything packed up by tomorrow, then I'll head out."

"Carson?" She heard him choke on the name.

"The private who I gave all my furniture to. It's a good thing Adam still had friends around here."

"Right." There was a pause and she took another sip of her beer before she heard Sam let out a long breath. "I'll see you Sunday."

"I'll be there." She felt as though she had to end with that promise because she wasn't sure he understood she'd be there. At this point she'd give anything to be with Sam, next to Sam, or under Sam rather than standing in her empty condo surrounded by lies.

Carson had arrived with another friend, another man who thought the world of Adam. They loaded all the furniture into Carson's truck and the truck of the friend.

Then they helped Amelia load up the car, fill it and her truck with boxes. She knew she was giving him all the furniture, but she bought them each a six pack too.

As she drove away from Atlanta, around one o'clock, with her life in boxes and Adam's car she'd have to sell, she let out a long and satisfying breath.

A quick text to Sam that she'd arrive very early Sunday morning and she was on her way to a new life. New friends. New career. New man. The last thought gave her chills. She just hoped he was as good a man as she thought he was. Or someone *was* going to end up with a broken nose.

~*~

It was still dark when Amelia pulled up in front of the townhouse on the far west side of Parson's Gulch around three in the morning. She was glad there weren't many cars on the street as the trailer on the back of her poor Blazer was taking up considerable space.

The neighborhood was quiet. She liked the peacefulness. She looked up toward the sky. The stars were so bright she felt as though she could reach up and grab one. The moon was just setting and in another hour the sun would be rising on what she hoped would be a beautiful Sunday morning.

"Are you planning on hanging out here in the street?" Sam's voice washed over her even though it was soft as if not to wake the neighbors.

"I wasn't sure about coming this early. I thought about just sleeping in the truck."

"Don't ever say that again." She could see the white of his teeth flash against the dark of the early morning.

"This is a wonderful place." She watched him walking toward her.

He was dressed casually in an old T-shirt and a pair of jeans. She thought he was sexy in his suit with his glasses on, but this topped it. His hair was rumpled and she knew he'd fallen asleep waiting for her and she didn't blame him.

As he grew near she could feel heat growing in her belly. In the glow of the streetlight and starlight his eyes focused in on hers. His lips parted as he moved right to her, wrapped an arm around her waist and wrapped his other hand into her hair.

His mouth came down on hers and that heat in her belly exploded through her entire body.

She braced her body against his, wrapping her arms around his neck, and deepening the kiss which had her head spinning.

Sam's hand slid down her back then both of his hands grasped her bottom and gave her another boost against his body. She let out a sensual grunt from her throat without leaving his lips and pulled him even closer.

"You want to do this?" he asked his lips still working against hers. "Please tell me you want to do this."

Amelia trailed a kiss down his throat and to his ear. "I haven't thought of anything else. Get me inside."

Sam hoisted her to his hips and carried her up the front steps as she continued trailing kisses across his mouth, cheeks, and neck.

When they reached the front door he pressed her to it. "Open it. Hurry."

She moved her mouth back to his and reached for the door handle behind her. When the door opened he nearly toppled them both inside, but with a stagger he caught them and she kicked the door closed behind them.

Sam turned them so that her back was pressed up against the door and his body was pressed against her.

She could feel every hard muscle under his shirt tense as he lowered her to her feet.

Her hands went to work tugging and lifting his T-shirt over his head. For a moment she scanned a look over his naked skin. Though she was used to men with bulging biceps and cut abs, the fine toned lines of Sam's body were welcoming—unthreatening.

His hands moved under her shirt. His fingers skimmed her skin sending tingles down her spine all the way to her toes. Never—and she knew it had been never—had she wanted a man this bad.

Sam pulled her T-shirt over her head and let it drop to the floor as his mouth opened to hers, engulfing her moans.

The cold door pressed against her bare skin as Sam's lips pressed against her collar bone.

"My room," he moved his lips to her ear. "We have to…" His hands began working on the button of her jeans. "My room."

Amelia pressed her hands against Sam's firm chest and gave him a push back. She scooped her hair back and moved past him.

"Upstairs?"

"Um, yeah. First door on the right."

She was halfway up the stairs when she turned back to him. "C'mon. I can't hold out much longer," she said.

Hunger flashed in his eyes as he hurried up behind her, scooped her up, and carried her into his bedroom.

Chapter Thirteen

Sam rolled onto his back. He swallowed hard trying to moisten his throat and suck in as much air as possible.

Amelia lay next to him panting for her own breath. Her skin was slicked with sweat and it glistened in the moonlight.

"Oh…God. That…was…"

"Freaking amazing," she finished his thought. "God damned, freaking amazing."

Sam chuckled. "I've never had it described like that."

"Trust me." She panted again. "A very accurate description."

Sam rolled to his side and looked down at her. She was perfect. Strong, toned, strong—he'd already thought that. But damn, she was the most beautiful woman he'd ever known. He ran a finger down her body, between her slickened breasts.

"You'll stay won't you?"

"I'm homeless. Of course I'll stay." She smiled up at him as she propped herself up on her elbows. "And tell me this luxury place of yours comes with food. You worked up an appetite in me." She rolled to face him. "And I could use some food."

He let the groan in his throat rattle out. "I could find you some food. Something tells me we could both use some energy."

Her eyes narrowed in a seductive wanting. "It's been awhile since I've had sex. I could go a few more times," she offered.

"I'll bet you've got me beat. I might wear you out. It's been a very long time for me."

Amelia rolled him to his back and straddled him. As she looked down, her hair curtaining her face, she ran her hands over his chest.

"How long?"

He blinked hard. "You really want to know that?"

"I think you've gotten a good grasp on the fact I'm not some petty and jealous woman."

"Oh I had a good grasp," he said as he gave her thighs a squeeze and she wiggled on top him.

"Seriously. How long."

Sam winced. "Do I get my man card pulled if I tell you it's been over a year—maybe more?"

Her lips tightened. "I won't pull your man card, but I don't believe you either."

He pushed her off of him and rolled her to her back. "Why?"

"Men don't go that long."

"Some believe if you have sex it means more than—well than just sex."

Her eyes widened. "This is more than just sex?"

Sam brushed her hair from her face and made sure he was looking her in the eye. "Yes."

She bit down on her lip and nodded. "Food. You promised me food."

Sam nipped her lip with a kiss and climbed from the bed. He held a hand out to her and pulled her to her feet. "I'll feed you, but you can't change."

"Pardon me?"

"You have to stay just like this," he said gazing at her perfect nakedness. "It's a deal breaker."

She shrugged and walked out of the bedroom.

Sam took a moment to let the rapid beat of his heart settle. To him it would always be more than just sex. Now he just had to convince her. At least she wasn't going away anytime soon. He'd have time.

He let out a breath. No woman had ever done this to him—ever made him feel this alive. It wasn't right that she'd only lost her husband and he'd been so obsessed with her he'd already taken her to bed.

What did that say about him?

He'd seen spouses do it before. It was a moment of weakness—a moving on before the true power of the grief hit. He'd always despised men who moved in on that weakness and now here he was—that man.

"Are you coming down?" Amelia called from the kitchen.

"Yeah, be right down."

He just had to wrap his mind around what he'd just done. The threat that his license could be pulled now for crossing the line wore heavy on his mind. Knowing the threat of what Amelia could do to him wore heavy on his heart.

Noise rattled from the kitchen. Cupboard doors being opened and closed. When he walked in she was standing there with the glow of the refrigerator light illuminating her naked body. She hadn't covered up. He bit back his smile, but it was there.

"What are you looking for?" he asked as he stood admiring.

"Food. You don't have any."

He rubbed the stubble on his cheeks. "You're right. Do I have milk?"

She pulled out a half of a gallon, smelled it, and nodded. "Yeah. That's all."

"I have cereal. I'll buy you lunch later. After a nap."

He moved to the cupboard and pulled down two bowls and then retrieved two spoons from a drawer.

Sam set them on the table and moved to another cupboard.

"I have Raisin Bran, Cap'n Crunch, Fruity Pebbles, Cocoa Pebbles, and Frosted Flakes."

A laugh burst from her and he turned. "Really? This is what a big time lawyer eats for breakfast?"

"I'm not big time."

"You're a professional."

"Kid at heart?"

She moved to him and quickly pressed her naked body against his. "Nothing about you says kid." She moved her lips against his. "Nothing."

She stepped back and examined her choices in the cupboard. "My mom would never let us have any of these. But when she was deployed we had our share." She smiled. "I'll be having some Frosted Flakes."

"I think that would be my choice too."

She gave him a wink, reached for the box, and headed back to the table.

They'd dined on cereal, had sex one more time, and then taken a long nap wrapped in each other's arms. When they'd awakened—they had sex once more, then took a long, hot shower.

Amelia was in post-stress heaven. However, she couldn't help but wonder if Sam thought she might be some shameless hussy. After all, she'd just buried her husband. Ex-husband. Lying, cheating, piece of crap husband. Solid soldier husband who saved the lives of a dozen men with the selfless act of dying for his country.

That part always got her.

She'd tossed on the clothes she'd traveled in and ran out to the street to get her clothes from her Blazer.

"Oh, Dear Lord!"

She heard him from the street and turned to see a bare chested Sam, in jeans and a pair of flip-flops, standing on the porch.

"A '69?"

She looked at her beat up Blazer, but as she looked back at him he was already walking toward the mustang on the back of the trailer.

"It's beautiful." He walked beside the trailer and looked at the car.

To her it was a car. An old car. Something that certainly shouldn't have cost Adam what it had, but Adam was a man of impulse. That would explain picking women up at bars, taking them home, and marrying three of them.

She realized she was grinding her teeth and unlocked her jaw as Sam climbed up onto the trailer.

"How many miles?"

Amelia shrugged. "I have no idea. We have to sell it. This is the car loan."

"This? That car loan is nearly seventy thousand dollars. I was expecting a gold plated Hummer."

"I don't know cars. I know how to kick the crap out of you in one if you pull any funny business. But I seriously don't care about cars."

"It's in mint condition. Minus the amount of boxes shoved in it." He gave her a look that said that might have been a mistake. But again—she didn't care.

"Seventy grand and it's yours."

After opening the door to the Blazer she pulled a duffle bag out of the front seat and swung it over her shoulder.

She noticed him wince at the price, but then she'd seen the flash of *maybe* in his eyes.

"It would look nice in your driveway for now though. Especially since I don't have anywhere to park it."

He nodded. "Sure. That's not a problem." He looked away from the car and back at her. "Did you tell Penelope and Vivian you were back in town?"

"No." She wasn't used to having to report to people. "How am I going to explain that I stayed here?"

"Right." He raked his hands through his sandy hair leaving trails where his fingers had gone. "I suppose we should get you a hotel room tonight and return your trailer."

"Sounds horrible." She walked toward him. "But yes. That is exactly what we should do."

Once more Sam drove to Oklahoma City and they returned the rental trailer. After the morning they'd had he figured they were in need of steak. So he found a steak house and they had a late lunch away from prying eyes.

"What do you suppose Adam's father wants to say to us?" she asked as she filled her mouth with a bite of steak stacked with a bite of potato.

Sam shrugged. "I'm assuming he wants to wrap his head around three wives."

"One wife. Two women with children."

Sam wiped his mouth. "It's all strange. But I'm an optimist. I think this is going to work out for the three of you. You're staying is giving those two some hope."

Amelia picked up her water and took a sip. "I think they could use that. I could use that," she said nearly under her breath.

He reached his hand across the table and covered hers. "You're going to tell them about us, aren't you? I can't keep hiding my feelings for you and eating in the city."

Her hand tensed under his and she slid it away. "When the time is right. We have a lot to think about first."

Sam nodded, retracted his hand, and cut off a piece of steak. He shoved it in his mouth.

Patience. A lawyer had patience. But damnit, he didn't want to hide.

He chewed on the piece of meat and thought. It had only been a week. One week. How stupid of him to have moved things along like he had.

He swallowed. Okay, she'd come to him. She'd been rolled up in those sheets as much as he had. But to her it was sex. To him it was a whole lot more.

Patience, he reminded himself one more time. It would all work out.

Chapter Fourteen

The Mustang had been parked in Sam's driveway and most of the boxes had been stored in his garage. She'd owe him for that.

Amelia settled herself on her bed, pillows propped up behind her, and an old Friends episode on the TV. She pressed Penelope's phone number and listened to the ring.

"Hello?" The kind and innocent voice answered and Amelia swallowed hard. She knew she was about to bust out a slew of lies.

"Hey, how's it going?"

"Oh, we're doing very well together. Vivian taught me how to make meatballs. Do you know how to do that? I've never cooked. Well nothing more than something that comes in a box."

Amelia let out a small laugh. The woman was unlike any she'd ever known.

"I'm glad it worked out. I just wanted to tell you I'm back in town. I got a hotel room for a few weeks. Sam says the lead on the town house is good, but we can't move in for a few weeks."

"Oh. Well, Vivian said I could stay here too. With her and the girls as long as I needed."

Amelia turned off the TV and sat up. "She did? And you're okay with that?"

She could hear a door close and Penelope's breath grew deeper as though she'd been walking. "I think she needs a friend. I don't think she has any."

"So you're bonding?"

"Yes," she said softly. "Adam's parents, well, his mother isn't too nice to Vivian. His dad is okay."

"What about her parents?"

"They live in Washington. Seattle. I guess she grew up in Parson's Gulch, but when she married Adam and moved away with him after his first deployment they moved."

"And he brought her back here?"

"I guess. She doesn't like to talk about it too much. I don't think she and Adam had a real good relationship."

Amelia thought that was obvious.

"If things are good, then I think you should stay with her. Did Sam tell you about meeting with his parents tomorrow?" she asked as she reclined back on the bed.

"I think it's just his dad. I hope it's just his dad. His mom scares me. I'm glad I'd never met them. I certainly don't think I would have married him."

The thought made Amelia stifle a laugh. "If you need me I'm here, okay?"

"Sure. I'll see you in the office tomorrow."

"Okay." Amelia hung up the phone.

It was petty of her to be so protective of Penelope— especially with Vivian. But there just was something that bothered Amelia about Vivian. She couldn't pin point it. She was nasty mean on Monday and by Wednesday was making them dinner. People didn't usually drop their barriers like that.

Then the thought struck her and she sat back up. What if the two of them were plotting against her? What if…

She actually laughed out loud. How stupid was that? Who cared? She didn't have anything more than they did. In fact she had the liability of that stupid car in Sam's driveway—not them.

Amelia had never been *girlie*. She'd never cared to be friends with other girls and she certainly would never have cared if they were spending time together without her. So why was she so worried about Vivian and Penelope?

It was petty. She was being stupid.

She clicked the TV back on and relaxed. But something still nagged at her and then she knew what it was. What if Penelope told Vivian about her and Sam? That would ruin Sam. Now she was a bit more understanding of her feelings.

She let out a breath. Good. It wasn't all estrogen based. That she could deal with.

~*~

It was already freaking hot, Sam thought as he made sure the conference room was ready for anything. He had boxes of tissue for crying women. He had extra bottles of water in the refrigerator and a carafe of coffee already filled with another pot brewing.

Leave it to his mother to need a day to shop before she moved—she had to choose this day.

Penelope and Vivian walked through the door together. He'd have to admit to himself it wasn't a sight he thought he'd ever see. The two of them smiling, together. Okay, the weekend together must have done them some good.

"Good morning, Sam," Vivian said and he made himself smile. The woman still scared him.

Penelope simply smiled then drew in a breath. "Good morning. Is your mother here?"

"She took the day off to shop. I expect you'll be fine. Other than this morning's meeting, we don't have too much going on today."

She nodded nervously. "I'll put my stuff in my desk and get the room set up."

"I already did that." He walked toward her. "Are you okay?"

"She's been throwing up all morning," Vivian said and the snide tone was back. Sam decided that made him more comfortable.

"The baby?" he asked softly.

"Some." Penelope rested her hand on her stomach. "The rest is nerves. I don't want his parents to hate me. And we didn't tell them who we were the other night. They probably want to sue us."

"They have nothing to sue you for."

She nodded with his answer, but it didn't change the fact that looking at her made him nervous.

"Where's Amelia?" Vivian asked looking around the office.

"I'm sure she'll be here soon. I haven't talked to her," Sam said with a clear conscience. He hadn't talked to her since she checked into the hotel room and they'd made love on her bed one more time.

The thought had him loosening his tie.

"She called Penelope last night. I know she's in town."

"Yes. She dropped Adam's car off at my house before she got a hotel room. She needed a place to store it."

Vivian narrowed her eyes. "I have a decent size lot. She could have brought it to my house."

Now his nerves were caught in his throat. "Yes. She could have, I suppose."

She ran her tongue over her teeth and gave him a nod.

The door to the office opened again and a man walked in. He could only assume this was Frank Monroe, Adam's father.

From what Sam could remember of Adam, this man shared many of the same strong features. And being ex-military, as he knew he was, the hair cut would have given that away.

"Hello, Frank," Vivian's voice was soft and shook just a bit.

"Viv." He acknowledged her with a nod. "And you're Penelope, right?" He shifted his glance.

"Yes, sir."

He let out a grunt and another nod before fixing his eyes on Sam.

"Mr. Jackson?"

Sam moved toward the man who stood a good four inches taller than he did. "Yes, sir. Sam Jackson."

Frank shook his hand. "Thank you for meeting me." Frank looked around the office. "There is one more, right? One more woman?"

"Yes, that would be me."

Amelia's voice came from behind the man. He stepped to the side and looked down at her.

"I'm Amelia." She held out her hand and shook it.

He cleared his throat. "You're the actual wife?"

"So they tell me. But we all share that title, sir." She looked toward Sam. "Are we ready?"

"Yes."

Sam showed them to the conference room. He noticed that when Amelia walked past him she didn't acknowledge him. It was best, but he didn't like it. A smile would have been nice.

The women all took the same seats they had the last time they'd met, but Frank took the seat Sam would usually occupy. So he sat next to Vivian.

"Mr. Monroe, is your wife coming?"

Frank Monroe rested his arms on the table and clasped his hands. "No. I asked her to stay home. She's very fragile right now and I'm not sure we'd accomplish much." He made eye contact with each woman. "Vivian told us about the predicament you're all in. I'm sure you can appreciate that as the father of a fine soldier this is very hard for me to believe."

Sam watched as Penelope forced herself to blink, Vivian looked down at the table, and Amelia met Frank's eyes. She rested her arms on the table in the exact same manner he had.

"Sir, I'm sure you also can appreciate that none of us were prepared for this. It came as quite a shock to all of us."

Frank made a noise as if he were sucking the words out from between his teeth. "I'm a big enough man to admit that men, and women, make some pretty amazing mistakes. I'd say that Adam did just that." He stood from his chair and paced the small space before him. "I'm not proud of what my son did. He was a good soldier. That doesn't always relate to being a good husband. Look at the house he had his family in. A providing husband would have taken better care."

That said a lot, Sam thought. At least the man wasn't candy coating his son to be someone they all knew he wasn't.

He walked around Sam and to the other side of Vivian, resting his hand on her shoulder. "Vivian stood by my son since high school. I have two beautiful granddaughters. I thank God for them. But she knows my wife has always had reservations against her."

Sam watched as Vivian wiped at her eyes. He pushed a box of tissue in front of her, but she refused it. Obviously in front of Adam's father tears were seen as weakness.

Frank moved to the other end of the table and rested his hands palm down. He took a breath. "I'll make this short and sweet. I have recently come into the knowledge that Adam wasn't necessarily responsible for getting in the paperwork for your marriage." He nodded toward Vivian.

"I can't condone what he did by marrying others when he should have at least honored the vows he made to you."

He was speaking to Vivian, but he kept his focus down.

"I'm told you're pregnant with my son's child as well?" He looked up and focused on Penelope until she met his eye.

"Yes. Yes, sir."

He gave her a slow nod. "Congratulations."

"Thank you," her voice was soft and she sounded fragile.

"You have my support."

Penelope's eyes grew wide. "I do? I—I mean, thank you."

Frank pulled out a chair and sat down. "Vivian also shared with us that the three of you are going to go into business together. She says that Adam's bills are more than what is expected from his insurance policies."

"I have those here if you'd…" Frank held a hand up to stop Sam.

"I'm aware of his habits. I find it admirable that three women who had an unfortunate relationship with the same man are willing to work together."

"Sir," Amelia spoke up. "Their children deserve the best. I'm sure you understand that. Adam isn't here to be part of their lives. At least the children will have each other."

"Like I said, that's admirable of you. Especially you." He looked at Amelia. "You could walk away and you haven't. I looked into you, you know. Your mother was a well decorated solider."

Amelia pushed back her shoulders. "Yes, sir, she was."

"It looks to me that she and your father raised a very fine woman."

Amelia batted her eyes rapidly. "Thank you, sir."

135

He nodded and pulled folded papers from his back pocket. He laid them on the table and flattened them out.

"I have decided that it is time my wife and I move from this area and retire. I have a hankering to own a boat and do some fishing. She…well she needs to separate herself from what's going on."

Frank picked up the papers and walked toward Sam. He handed him the papers and took his original seat.

"My mother lived right in town. The house is on Main and Pine. The house itself is about one hundred and ten years old. It needs paint, some updated wiring, and the floors could be redone." Frank rubbed his hand over his mouth then clasped them together. "I've rented the house out over the years. I've used the garage for storage as well as the attic. But the yard is enormous. The living space on the second floor is very roomy. And I think the main area would be a wonderful place for a daycare facility."

All three women raised their heads and their eyes focused on Frank Monroe's.

Sam looked down at the papers Frank had handed him. "Sir, this is the deed to the property."

"Yes. I'm signing it over to the ladies. I guess specifically to Amelia as she's the heir to Adam's estate, but it's for all of you. I know you'll have to put into it before you can open, but this is what I can do for my grandchildren." He then looked at Amelia. "And my son's wife."

The air in the room grew thicker and Vivian's sobs were now only matched by Penelope's. But it was Amelia who stood and walked to Frank.

He stood and looked down at her.

"Sir, this is very unselfish. I'm not sure thank you is adequate."

She moved into him and wrapped her arms around him. Frank arms tensed before he embraced her, then he stepped back and cleared his throat.

He pulled a set of keys from his pocket. "Here are the keys. Anything left in the house is yours as well. You can keep it. Sell it. Donate it. I have what I needed." Frank turned to Sam. "I want to make sure you're financially set for taking care of all this above what the insurance will pay you. I know you've been helping these fine women out. I appreciate that."

Sam stood. "I'm taken care of, sir." Telling him that he was hoping to be an integral part of their lives for a long time was probably not appropriate.

Frank gave another nod and pursed his lips. "Vivian," he said and waited for her to look up. "I'm sorry for all the years of pain my wife might have caused you. Adam was her light. When his focus became you…well…I'm sure you understand."

"I do."

"You're doing a fine job with the girls. I'm very proud of them. And you."

Vivian stood. "Thank you, sir. That means a lot."

"You'll let us visit when we are in town?"

"Of course."

"And you'll keep us updated about the girls?"

She nodded. "Yes."

"Okay." He tucked his hands into his front pockets. "I guess that's all."

He turned to leave but Vivian moved and stopped his exit.

"Thank you. You have no idea what comfort this brings to me to have your support and this gift." She sniffed back her tears. "I loved Adam. I did. With all my heart from the moment I met him. I never could have seen this coming, but I loved him. And you've always been there for me and the girls. I appreciate that. This gift will take care of them—us—for a long time." She moved in and kissed him on the cheek.

When she stepped back he cleared his throat again.

"Vivian has my cell phone number if you all need anything."

He moved past her and left the office.

Sam looked down at the papers in front of him. "This is official. The three of you now jointly own the house at Main and Pine."

"It's a wonderful house," Vivian said softly. "His wife always wanted to live there."

"They never moved in?" Amelia asked.

"He wouldn't let her live in his mother's home." Vivian smiled then tucked her lips between her teeth as if she were hiding it. "Frank Monroe is a man of his word. If he said he'd marry a woman it would be for life—even if he decided later she wasn't who he thought she was."

Penelope looked up at her. "She scares me."

"Don't let her. Frank would never let her do anything to harm you. And she wouldn't. She might make it hard on you, but she wouldn't hurt you."

Vivian picked up the keys and held them in her hand.

"What do you say we go check out our new business location?"

Sam watched as Vivian's cheeks lifted and lightness danced in her eyes. Frank Monroe might have just made up for his son's shortcomings.

But if Sam remembered the house correctly, these women had a lot of work ahead of them. He knew a thing or two about home improvements. This might just be his excuse to get more involved.

AMELIA

He looked toward Amelia who seemed to be deep in thought. What possibly could have happened between the time he left her bed and now?

Chapter Fifteen

The three women stood in front of the house looking up. The white picket fence in the front yard was falling apart and the gate hung by only one hinge.

Paint peeled from the house, the mail box stood at an angle, and the windows had a hundred-year fog covering them.

Penelope shifted a glance between Vivian and Amelia. "I'll bet it was lovely."

Amelia looked toward Vivian who was smiling. "It is." She looked at them. "C'mon, it's old. It needs some love, but look at the possibilities." Her voice was airy and full of promise, but Amelia looked back at the house and didn't see it.

"Maybe we'd better go in and look," she offered and Vivian headed toward the door.

Moving the broken gate, Vivian waited for the others to catch up to her. She took each step of the porch slowly as they creaked beneath her.

Taking the keys from her pocket, she slid it into the lock on the door.

"Okay, here we go." She turned the lock and pushed open the door.

The three women stepped in and stood silently.

Vivian had been right. The inside was amazing—or might have been a hundred years ago.

The entry gave to a hallway and a set of stairs. To each side of the entry there were enormous rooms.

"I think this one was the dining room." Vivian pointed to the left. "And over here was the sitting room, living room, it goes back to the library. But it all circles around to the kitchen. The whole floor flows." She walked toward the sitting room. "There are these," she began to pull a large wooden door from the wall. "Pocket doors."

"Oh, my!" Penelope's eyes opened wide. "Look how beautiful they are."

"They're original," Vivian said as she pushed it back into place.

The three of them walked through the house in a huddle. Each room had some furniture, the floors were bare, and the air thick with Oklahoma red dust.

Vivian had something to say about each room. She'd remembered being there when Adam's grandmother had been alive. "It was this dusty then too," she snickered.

The kitchen was a different story. Where the other rooms had been left in their nearly natural state, the kitchen had been remodeled sometime in the 1970's.

Amelia laughed. "Is that an avocado green refrigerator?"

"I'm sure it doesn't work," Vivian said.

"I'd be afraid to see what lived in it."

The walls had orange and brown patterns. The light fixture over the eating area was citrine glass. The mosaic tile of the back splash was—well—hideous, Amelia thought.

"If we use this for the daycare center this will all have to be industrial," Amelia offered.

"Thank God!" Penelope burst out, then covered her mouth. "Sorry." She looked at Vivian. "The house is wonderful."

Vivian let out a laugh. "It's horrible. But it's free. Free is good."

"It's going to cost a lot to fix it," Amelia added.

"Yep. But can't you see what it could be?"

Amelia couldn't, but she'd seen what Vivian had done with the shack she lived in. She could only imagine that tucked into her pocket there were rose colored glasses. But

AMELIA

Amelia would just have to take Vivian's word on it. To her, a bulldozer seemed more appropriate.

They started up the stairs to the second level. Each step creaked under them.

"These are safe aren't they?" Penelope asked.

"You're fine," Vivian said as she brushed cobwebs from in front of her.

The second floor had four bedrooms. One shared a Jack and Jill bathroom. The other two had a bathroom down the hall.

"I'm guessing these bathrooms might have been old closets?" Amelia said as she looked inside. She realized that the bathroom in her small condo had been twice the size of the one she was looking at.

"Remember how old it is," Vivian said, her voice still dancing with enthusiasm.

Penelope pointed to the ceiling. "What's that?"

"You pull it down and it's stairs to the attic. There's just junk up there if I remember right. We'll go through it some other time."

They made their way back downstairs and then to the basement. There wasn't much there but a furnace that took up most of the space.

When they were back on the main floor they stood in the entry and all looked around in different directions.

Amelia didn't know what to make of it. She didn't even know where they'd begin. Penelope, she knew, would just go along with whatever anyone told her. Vivian, on the other hand, wore a smile of satisfaction as if she could see every detail.

One thing was for sure, this would give them some bonding time and perhaps some healing time too.

Amelia hadn't known she'd needed it until she'd spoken to Penelope on the phone the night before. Now, she ached for it.

~*~

Sam paced the floor in his kitchen with his cell phone in his hand. The three of them had headed toward the old house around eleven o'clock and it was now six. He hadn't heard anything from Amelia. It was beginning to kill him.

He'd brought her contact information up on his screen four times already with anticipation of hitting the call button. He'd written six texts, but he hadn't sent them.

There was no reason he couldn't just go over to her hotel. Just a friendly invite to dinner—right?

Stalker. He was becoming a stalker.

Sitting at the kitchen table he rested his head on his hand. There was an ache that consumed him when he thought of her. How could a man like Adam Monroe not want to be with her all the time? What could drive a man away from her?

Another hour passed and there still had been no call or text. He couldn't wait anymore. He picked up his phone and just as he pushed the button to call her, the phone rang in his hand.

"Hello?" He was too anxious. He was going to sound desperate.

"Hi." Her voice was soft and hollow. "Are you home?"

"Yeah." He tried to sound casual. "Is everything okay?"

"I just need you. If that's alright."

He almost asked if it was really Amelia on the phone. He couldn't imagine the woman he was involved with could sound so broken.

"I'll be here. Come over any time."

"Thanks."

The line went dead. He tucked his phone into his pocket and walked to the refrigerator for a beer. Just as he twisted off the top his doorbell rang.

He stood there for a moment and contemplated even answering it. He wanted his evening free for Amelia.

As he walked to the door he took a sip of his beer. She'd called him. She needed him. That had given him a warm feeling throughout his body. He could do with being needed.

He was more than a little surprised to find Amelia standing on the doorstep.

"I'm sorry," she started and that alone threw him. She wasn't one to apologize easily. "I was parked out front."

"You could have just come to the door." He stepped back and let her through.

"I didn't want to bother you."

Sam shut the door and turned to touch her arm. "You could never be a bother to me."

Amelia looked at his beer. "Can I have one of those?"

"Sure." He handed her the one in his hand. "I just opened this."

She accepted it and took a long pull from it. "Thanks. Are you alone?"

Sam narrowed his gaze. "Of course. Who would be here?"

"I don't know. I've only been around this town a week. I don't know what history you have with anyone. I don't know who Adam has or hasn't pissed off. People know I'm new in town, but as of yet they haven't figured out who the hell I am, but with three of us toting around the same last name…" she blew out a breath. "I guess I have a lot on my mind."

"Do you want to sit down and talk? I have some left over spaghetti from lunch I was going to warm up for dinner. I'd share."

Her eyes softened as she smiled. "I'd like that."

Sam took her hand in his, interlaced their fingers, and walked her to the kitchen.

Amelia sat down at the table and drank from her beer. Sam took out the leftovers and another beer for himself.

"So how was the house?" he asked as he put the spaghetti into a bowl.

"It's decrepit, but Vivian sees great promise in it."

"That's good, right?"

"Sure. I don't see it, but as long as she does."

Sam hit the buttons on the microwave and turned back to her. "I've been known to get my hands dirty. I'd be happy to help you all out when you're ready to dig in."

Amelia laughed as she pressed the bottle to her lips. "You've done a project like this before?"

So, she did think he was only a nerd. He knew that look. "You'd be surprised what I can do if you give me time to show you."

Her eyes grew darker with his statement. It was a look he appreciated more than the dazed and confused one she'd walked in with.

When the microwave beeped, Sam carefully took out the bowl. He divided it into two more bowls, dug forks from the drawer, and set one bowl in front of her.

"Thanks."

He sat down in the chair next to her. "You know I can cook a decent meal." He grinned. "When I have groceries that is. Maybe this weekend we could grill something."

She licked her lips. "I'd really like that."

Sam twirled his spaghetti on his fork and watched as she pushed hers around in the bowl.

146

"So, what's got you so upset?"

Amelia's head snapped up and he suddenly wasn't sure he liked the way he'd posed the question. A moment later she was looking at the bowl again.

"I have all these girlie emotions running through me and I don't know what the hell to do with them."

Sam stopped chewing and watched her. Swallowing hard he picked up his beer and took a sip.

"I've had the opportunity to get to know you *really well*. Under all of those sleek muscles, you're all girl. What part of that can't you handle?"

She let out a grunt of a laugh then set her fork in the bowl and rested her elbows on the table.

"Last night when I was talking to Penelope on the phone she sounded so…content. I told her I got us a room until the townhouse was ready, but she's happy with Vivian."

"But that's good."

"Yes. I got jealous. I mean…me…I don't do that."

Sam tried not to smile, but he couldn't help it. "It's okay. You and Penelope bonded, why shouldn't she bond with Vivian?"

"Because I haven't." She picked up her beer and took a long drink. "She said she thought they were becoming friends and she thought Vivian needed one. Well for some reason it chapped my hide. It was dumb. It was petty, but it ate at me all night."

"Is that why you were so short this morning with everyone?"

Amelia shrugged her shoulders. "I talked to Penelope before we got to your office. I told her that today we should look for a doctor." She let out a sigh. "I guess Vivian took her to her doctor on Friday when I was in Atlanta. The baby is doing great."

Sam reached for her hand. "Honey…"

"I'm fine." She pulled her hand back. "I told you. I don't know what to do with all of this." She took a fork full of noodles and shoved them in her mouth. "She's nearly through her first trimester," she said while chewing. "In six months there will be another of Adam's babies in this world."

"And he or she will be born to a loving mother."

"I know. Son-of-a-bitch, she doesn't deserve to do this alone."

God, he just wanted to scoop her up and hold her. She was out of sorts. At that moment he was grateful to have had two older sisters too.

"She's not alone. She has the two of you," he said softly. "You're not going to let her down."

"I know that Vivian's girls will love the baby too. She's trying to decide how to tell them that the baby is their sister or brother."

"She'll figure it out in time."

Amelia took another bite and then another. Sam smiled as he took a drink from his beer. "Feeling a little better?"

"I don't know. I hate even getting worked up over any of it."

"You're entitled." He reached for her hand again and this time she locked fingers with him. "Stay tonight."

"I don't…"

"I know. You don't think it's a good idea. But you're going to tell Vivian about us anyway, right?"

She bobbed her head around. "Yes," she finally said, but the tone was more in agreement toward him and not the sigh of an answer from a woman who believed it.

"There is an us that goes deeper than bed, right?"

"Sam…"

"I've been clear about that, now you need to be." His voice rose higher than he'd have liked it to, but he didn't want to be used any more than she did.

"I'll tell her," Amelia snapped out.

"That's not my point anymore. Tell me I'm not just someone you're using to forget what your husband did to you."

Her eyes opened wide and she ripped her hand from his. "Is that what you think?"

"I'm not getting much feedback to prove me wrong."

"I fell in love with a man once and look where that got me."

Sam let out a laugh. "I don't see it landing you anywhere you didn't choose to stay. You had a home. You had other *acquaintances* in Atlanta. Hell you have one freaking nice ride if you want it." He motioned toward the driveway with his hand.

"Acquaintances? Are you kidding me?" She was on her feet now and he followed right behind her.

"All I know is when you're around me I can't think straight. My body gets all crazy. My mind buzzes. I sit here waiting for you to call." He hadn't meant to say that part. She didn't need to know he waited for her. "You're not the only one who's been in love before and gotten screwed over or it didn't work out. I may not have had sex with anyone else in over a year, but I've been in love before. And this is better. Which leads me to believe that I'm…"

She pressed her hand to his mouth to stop him from talking.

"Don't. Don't you go there."

He pulled her hand down. "Why not?"

"Just don't." Amelia picked up her beer, finished it, and set it back down. "I should go."

"Fine."

Her eyes grew wide as if she hadn't expected him to agree.

"Thanks for dinner." She turned and walked to the door.

There was something now that buzzed through him and it was totally different. As much as he wanted her there, wanted her to sleep in his arms and to make love to her all night, he had to let her walk away.

He knew it wasn't forever, but as the door closed behind her, he felt sick.

Time. She needed time. Even though she might not admit it, she was a mourning widow. But Sam had no intentions of being the transitional person.

Chapter Sixteen

Vivian had dropped the girls off at the recreation center's drop-in daycare and then made a stop at Sam's office. He was in a cross mood and he wondered if either of the women in his presence would know why.

"Everything is signed over with the house. You officially own it. It's zoned for both business and residential. You'll have some taxes due on it soon." He swallowed hard. "I can help you with that if you need me to. I also have a friend who would like to look at the car. I told him to come by and see it since it's still in my driveway and has been for a week."

He said a little oath in his head. Now they knew he was upset as they exchanged looks.

"I should have moved it to my house," Vivian said. "I'm sorry it's in your way."

"It's not. I'm having a Monday, that's all." He pulled his glasses off and rubbed the bridge of his nose. "I had told Amelia I could come help at the house too. I've done my share of home improvements."

The women exchanged looks again. "She mentioned that," Vivian said. "She's been working on the fence out front and the yard. She said if we gave it some curb appeal we'd feel better about walking in the front door."

Sam smiled. "She's right." He sat back in his chair. "The owner of the garden shop is an old friend. I think maybe I'll pay her a visit and drop by some bedding plants. She hasn't planted anything yet has she?"

Penelope shook her head. "It's been really hot."

"I'll find something hearty."

Vivian looked at her watch. "I have to get the girls." She stood from her seat. "This drop in daycare stuff is nice.

I think we should offer it," she said toward Penelope as she picked up her purse and walked out of the office.

Penelope moved to stand, then instead leaned back in her chair and placed her hands on her stomach.

Sam lurched forward. "Is everything okay?"

Penelope smiled. "I'm still just the slightest bit queasy sometimes. I don't know why they call it morning sickness. I have it all day." She rubbed her stomach again. "It's fun though. I don't feel alone. I always have someone with me. I always have Adam with me." Her voice trailed off.

He'd seen Amelia break down. It was obviously Penelope's turn.

"Do you miss him?" he asked and Penelope nodded. "It's okay."

"I know. I just feel bad breaking down in front of the other two. Vivian loved him for a long time, but she really was without him most of their marriage. She's angry that he lied to her from day one." She continued to rub her stomach. "Amelia, well," she gave him a look of consideration before she continued. "I just think she's always got a chip on her shoulder."

Sam sat forward in his chair and rested his chin on his fist.

"Why do you think she's like that?"

Penelope shrugged. "I know her mom died when she was young."

"Sniper in Desert Storm."

Her eyes widened. "She didn't tell us that."

"Army brat. She's been around it her whole life."

Penelope bit down on her lip, looked at the floor, and then back up at him. "You haven't seen her lately have you?"

Sam sat back again. "We had a disagreement."

"I'm sorry."

"It wasn't over you. No need to be sorry."

Penelope knit her fingers together. "She asked about you last night. Wanted to know if you were doing okay."

"She did?"

She nodded. "Vivian thinks Amelia likes you so she's distancing herself from you because it's in bad taste."

Sam clenched his jaw. "In bad taste?"

"Since you're Adam's lawyer."

Crap, he thought as he ran his hand over his forehead.

Penelope leaned in toward the desk. "I didn't tell her you had kissed," she whispered and then sat back.

Dear Lord, if only Penelope knew what he'd done.

"Thanks for that." Sam picked his glasses back up and put them on. "I'd better get back to preparing these," he said stacking the papers on his desk into a pile. Can you set up a meeting with Mr. Hanover about his will? He wanted to update it now that he has three grandchildren."

Penelope stood. "I'll get right on that." She walked to the door and turned around "She'll be at the house until six. Then she'll be at the recreation center teaching a self-defense class and a kick boxing class."

"She got a job?"

Penelope nodded and then walked away.

That, he thought, was a positive sign. She had a job that meant she was staying in town.

~*~

It was eleven o'clock and the temperature had already gone over one hundred degrees. Sam's truck blew cold air inside, but he knew the wall of heat waited on the outside.

Amelia was in the front yard of the house on Main and Pine. She had a bandana wrapped around her head and her long, dark hair pulled up in a pony-tail. Her shorts were—

well—short and it showed off the magnificent sculpture of her legs. She had on a tank top and that too showcased those shoulders he missed.

In the bed of his truck he had a peace offering of sorts—a bush for the front walk and some flower baskets for the porch. They were God awful expensive, so he thought he'd start there.

She looked up over her sunglasses as he parked his truck in front of the house and stepped out into the wall of heat he knew could engulf a man and send him to his grave.

"It's looking nice. You fixed the gate and painted the fence."

Amelia looked at him, pushed her sunglasses back up, and kept raking up the dead grass.

Silent treatment. He was a lawyer, he was used to this.

Sam pulled down the tailgate of the truck and pulled the bush to the edge and then picked up the hanging baskets.

"I brought you some things for the yard."

She watched as he carried the baskets through the open gate and up to the porch. He smiled as he headed back to the truck for the bush.

When he turned around she was gone and the screen door was shutting on the front of the house.

What in the hell was wrong with her? Was she really going to be a whiney little girl? It didn't fit her. She wasn't the kind to throw a fit and…he stopped berating her in his mind when he picked up the bush and noticed her come out of the house. She had two glasses of iced tea in her hands.

Sam carried the bush to the walk, set it down, and then wiped the back of his hand over his sweat laden brow.

"Jesus, it's hot out here. How can you stand it?" he asked.

"Hydration. Drink." She handed him a glass and took the other for herself.

"Thanks." He tried to only sip, but he couldn't help but down the golden liquid. "Guess that hit the spot."

She smiled—actually smiled. "C'mon. I have a pitcher in the house in the new fridge."

She led the way into the house. Sam took a moment to take it all in. First of all it was hot as hell in there. She had all the windows open and no fans going. All of the furniture in each of the rooms had been pushed into the center of each room and draped with a drop cloth.

He followed her around to the kitchen and then stopped in his tracks. "Oh-my-God!"

She chuckled at his response. "Repulsive, isn't it?"

"I feel like I just went back in time, minus the new stainless steel refrigerator."

"Other one was the first thing we hauled out. It was avocado green."

"Of course." He looked around at the tile, the cabinets, the citrine lighting fixture above his head. "I didn't realize you girls would have so much work to do. I knew it was old, but..."

"It's fine. It was free and we'll make it work. Point is the girls will be with Vivian most of the time and Penelope will have her baby with her. Eye on the prize."

Right, eye on the prize.

She pulled the pitcher out of the new refrigerator and filled his glass.

"Thank you," he said trying not to hurry though this glass.

"Would you like a tour?"

Conversation. This was a bonus. "Sure. Is it as hot upstairs?"

"Worse."

He took a sip of tea. "Okay then."

She showed him through the house explaining the main floor and what they'd thought of for the set up. A play area here, infants there, lunch room here. It was basic and laid out just right.

The stairs creaked under his feet and he thought perhaps new treads were in order. He could look into doing that for them.

There was a lot he could do for them.

"What are you going to do with the bedrooms?" he asked.

"I'm not sure. Penelope doesn't have anywhere to live right now. We thought about once the house is livable she could stay here."

"What about you?" he said quietly. "You deserve to stay too."

"We'll see." She moved to go back down the steps.

"What's up there?" Sam turned and pulled the rope to the attic stairs and they came crashing down on top of him hitting him right across the chest and knocking him down.

"Sam!" He heard her voice ring out and a moment later she was next to him, on the floor, her hands already pulling open his shirt. "Are you okay? Talk to me."

"Ow! Freaking ow!" He said trying to sit up, but finding it very difficult.

"Don't move."

"Not a problem," he said as she opened his shirt.

"You're going to have one hell of a bruise."

"And here I thought it would be you that kicked the crap out of me." He tried to laugh, but that hurt too.

"Let's get you downstairs and get some ice on that." She helped him to his feet and then wrapped his arm around her shoulders and hers around his waist.

They took the stairs slowly and as they did the front door opened. A more than surprised Vivian walked in with a grocery bag in her hands.

"What are the two of you doing?" She asked in what Sam would definitely call an accusing voice.

"Sam pulled the door to the attic open and the stairs came right out on his chest. Help me get him to the kitchen to sit down."

The expression on Vivian's face changed to one of concern. She set the bag on the floor and moved to Sam.

She took his other arm and draped it over her neck and together they helped him to the kitchen.

He was sure he could have walked with less jarring to his chest, but they were being friendly.

They stopped in front of the only chair at an old table in the kitchen. "Sit down," Amelia ordered.

He did, but not with ease. She was right, he was going to have one hell of a bruise.

Amelia made him a makeshift bag of ice out of a plastic grocery bag. She wrapped a rag around it and handed it to him. "Put this on your chest."

He pressed it to his skin and pulled it away. "Damn, that hurts more."

Vivian snickered. "It's a good thing you don't give birth."

Sam narrowed his eyes at her and pressed it back to his chest.

"The yard looks nice," Vivian said as she walked to the counter to unload the items in her bag.

"Sam brought us a bush and some hanging plants," Amelia said sending him a glance he couldn't read.

"Thanks." Vivian turned and gave him an equally unreadable look.

"Like I said, I'd like to help out. The stairs need new treads. I could do that."

"You can?" Vivian pulled out a box of juice pouches and set them on the table.

"Yeah." He heard the sound of kids out back and he turned to see the enormous yard beyond the windows. "I didn't realize the yard was so big."

"It'll be a good playground," Vivian said with a smile. "The girls already love it. They're safe out there and I can work on the house."

"That's nice," Sam said turning back to them and noticing that both women watched the girls and smiled. "I suppose I should head back to work. I just wanted to drop off the plants before you headed to work," he said to Amelia.

"How did you...Penelope?"

"She said you were working at the recreation center. That's great."

"It'll do for now."

Sam stood, slowly. He tried to adjust in any direction that wouldn't cause him pain, but that wasn't working too well.

"Thank you for the flowers and bush," Vivian said as she prepared a snack for the girls.

"My pleasure."

He buttoned up his shirt and Amelia watched.

"I'll walk you out," she said and he figured that was progress.

He headed for the door with her behind him. "I have a guy coming to look at the Mustang."

"Good."

"Everything is official with the house. It's all yours."

"That's good too."

They walked through the small gate and out to his truck. "Well. Thank you for the tea."

"You're welcome."

He opened the door to his truck and slammed it shut as he turned back to her. "Are you really going to let this go like this?"

"Like what?"

"You haven't seen me or spoken to me in a week."

"I haven't seen you stop by and offer up an apology either."

He sucked in a breath to speak and then thought better of it. "I'm sorry."

"No you're not. You have no idea what you even said to hurt my feelings." She tucked her thumbs into the front pocket of her shorts. "I assume you need a twist in the sheets."

"Oh, honey. Now I think you should apologize." He turned back and opened the door to his truck. "I can wait for it."

"I don't apologize when I'm not wrong."

"Fine. Then let's have dinner and see who caves."

"Who caves?"

"Sure. Either one of us will apologize for God I have no idea what, or we'll twist in the sheets. I know how you feel about sex. You know how I feel about it."

"You want dinner?" Her sandaled foot tapped on the hot cement.

"I'll even buy." He smiled hoping it would seal the deal.

"I'll let you buy me dinner, but I'm not sleeping with you."

"That's fine by me. I'll be by tomorrow after work to start on the stairs too. But tonight I'll meet you at the hotel and I'll pick you up. Like a real date. Eight o'clock?"

She grunted between her teeth. "Fine."

"Fine." He gave her a nod and climbed into his truck. A moment later he was headed away from her, but he wore a grin. She was still fuming and she didn't even know why now. But, with a few of those kisses they could heat up and she'd loosen up. And when she did he'd move in and tell her what he'd tried to tell her the last week when she'd walked out on him.

He wasn't one to play with words just to gain access to someone. But he'd damn well use them if he felt they were true and that someone might feel the same way. And he was sure she did feel the same way. A man knew when a woman was more than just sex. He would seriously assume a woman would know that too. Of course it wouldn't be the first time he'd looked like an ass telling a woman he loved her. That had been the last mistake of his last relationship.

Well, hell. He thought better of it for a moment. Maybe he'd wait until he was really sure. There was no way to be sure she wouldn't high tail it out of town.

Yeah, he needed to win her over. He'd start with dinner.

Sam turned to head back to the office. Now he needed to get to his computer and Google "staircase repair" before he tried his hand at it tomorrow.

Chapter Seventeen

Amelia picked the rake back up and began assaulting the ground. She was still pissed at him, only now it was worse because she couldn't quite remember why she was so pissed at him.

She pulled the bandana from her head and wiped her face then tucked it into her pocket. The sun was too hot. The air was too thick. And damnit, if she didn't get a handle on her emotions she'd heat stroke.

"Need a bottle of water?" Vivian stood in the doorway with one in her hand, her arms crossed over her chest.

"I could use one, thanks."

Vivian walked across the porch and down the steps. She handed it to her, but continued to stand there with her arms crossed and her hip cocked.

Amelia thought this might be her natural look, which would only enhance the years to come when Amelia was forced to look at it.

"I have a shovel or another rake if you want…"

"What's going on with you and the lawyer?"

Amelia kept her face as casual as she could. "He stopped by with flowers and a bush."

"That's not what I mean and you know it." She stepped closer to her. "What's going on?"

Amelia gripped the handle of the rake in her hand. "Why don't you tell me what you think is going on?"

"I think you're making away with Adam's money."

Amelia let out a laugh at that. "You've seen the papers. I'm stuck with his debt. He had no money."

"Then why get so clingy with the lawyer?"

"He's a nice guy."

"Cute too, but you're walking a fine line making eyes at him."

"Wouldn't you consider him your friend?" Amelia shot back at Vivian.

"He's been nice enough to go above and beyond. Now I want to know why."

"He's a nice guy."

Vivian took one more step toward her and Amelia let the rake fall to the ground. "You're not the kind of woman who goes for nice guys."

"We at one point seemed to have the same taste in men. I'd have to assume you don't like nice guys either."

"This isn't about me. It's about you."

"What the hell does it matter if I flirt with the lawyer? He's-a-nice-guy," she bit out as Vivian grew even closer.

"What do you get out of it? Huh? What are the benefits to making moves on him? If you have Adam's debt and we secured the house then why the hell is he still coming around here bringing stuff? Why would you care to walk him to his truck and why the hell did you take Adam's car to his house and not to mine? If we're partners in all this crap how come you're so smooth with him?"

"Because I'm sleeping with him!" She finally let the words fly and Vivian stumbled back as though Amelia had actually hit her. "That's right. I don't give a damn about the man who I married and who screwed me and you over. I was over him when I found out about you and you can sure as hell guarantee I was over him when I found out about Penelope. But it isn't any of your goddamned business who I go to bed with."

"Oh, I think when you're nailing the lawyer in charge of everything…"

"He's done his work. Now he's Penelope's boss and the guy who is going to come and fix your staircase tomorrow so you don't fall though the wood."

"I'm supposed to believe that there isn't any perk for you?"

Amelia fisted her hands on her hips. "Sure. I'm not lonely. Maybe you should get laid and then you wouldn't be so miserable either."

"Oh!" Vivian charged at her and Amelia simply moved letting Vivian fall to the ground.

"You don't want to try that again. I taught your husband that being on the ground is the wrong place to be during a fight."

Vivian stared at her and then the tears came and then the sobs.

"You trained Adam?" She managed through breaths.

"Yeah. I trained him. Trained him how to take an ass whooping."

Vivian stared at her for a moment and then a laugh escaped. She covered her mouth with her hand then lowered it slowly. "Did you really kick his ass?"

"Yeah." The image rushed through her mind and then she laughed. Amelia sat down on the ground next to Vivian. "He was volunteering to be an attacker at an Army wives' training I was having. He got cocky and I put him in his place." She'd leave what happened next out of the story. "Then when we were married and I found out about you I broke his nose."

Vivian laughed again and then covered her mouth— again. "You didn't?"

"I did too. He pissed me off. Of course it didn't stop him. That's when he went to the bar, picked up Penelope's friend and took her home."

Vivian's shoulders dropped. "What about Penelope?"

Amelia pulled the one live piece of grass from the Earth and wrapped it around her finger. "They were married before he took her to bed."

"Really?"

Amelia nodded. "She was a virgin and he waited for her."

Vivian wiped at her eyes. "She's never been with anyone else?"

"No."

Vivian sighed. "Neither have I."

Amelia laughed. She didn't mean to, but she couldn't help it. "Okay. It's official. You and Penelope are going to my self-defense class and then my kickboxing class. You're going to learn to get your frustrations out with your fists and then at some point we'll get you laid."

The roll of laugher came from Vivian and she even lay back in the dirt that was once a yard. Penelope drove up in front of the house and hurried out of her car.

"Are you two okay?" She tore off her shoes and hurried toward them. "What happened?"

Amelia nodded toward Vivian. "She threatened me."

"What?"

Vivian laughed and sat up. "I don't think I was a threat."

"You charged at me."

"And I'm the one that landed on my butt."

Penelope held her hands up. "Why are you fighting? Why are you laughing?"

Amelia was sure Penelope was going to burst into tears. "Adam was a son-of-a-bitch."

"Oh," Penelope pursed her lips. "We can't keep thinking that." She placed her hands on her stomach.

"You do what you want. I'm going to think it." Amelia pushed to her feet and held a hand out for Vivian. "C'mon. You're going to my classes tonight. Both of you."

Penelope's eyes grew wide. "I can't. The baby."

"Is the size of a grapefruit, maybe." She really didn't know. "You're not going to go crazy, but you're coming."

"She's going?" She pointed to Vivian.

"She needs too. She just found out I'm sleeping with Sam."

"You are?" Penelope's eyes were as wide as when she'd seen them kiss.

Amelia walked toward her and rested a hand on her shoulder. "You understand how this adult thing happens, right? Did you think we'd stop with a kiss?"

Vivian walked up to both of them. "She saw you kiss him?" She turned to Penelope. "You saw them."

"I...well...oh, please don't put me on the spot." Penelope dropped her shoulders. "Yes. I saw them move in for a kiss. But I didn't know they..."

Amelia let out a grunt. "You two are prudes. We have to fix that."

"C'mon now," Vivian held up her hands. "We're the two that got knocked up by the same guy."

The smile tugged at Amelia's face nearly enough to hurt, but the astonished look on Penelope's brought the laughter between her and Vivian to a roll.

Vivian pulled Penelope into her arms and hugged her. "We are prudes. We've only been with Adam and now we're stuck with each other. We have to laugh."

"I can't laugh."

"Yes you can. We need to." Vivian looked at Amelia. "Let her be the slut. We have our kids."

Amelia brushed them off with a wave of her hand and headed for the house. "You two are jealous I got the lawyer first."

"I could make a play for him," Vivian called out.

"Nope. I'm pretty confident tonight he's going to try and tell me he loves me."

Vivian and Penelope looked at each other and then ran up the stairs following Amelia.

Who'd have thought they'd bond over her sleeping with the lawyer?

Chapter Eighteen

The night was too damn hot to dress up, but Amelia felt the need to dress to impress. After she'd drug Vivian and Penelope to her class and brought Ava and Emma in to kick the heavy bags for fun, she'd hurried back to the hotel.

She'd wanted to go buy something fun and flirty, but there hadn't been any time. So a relaxed pair of jeans and a gauze tank top that belted at the waist was as impressive as Sam was going to get.

The knock at the door came promptly at eight. He wouldn't be anticipating her change in mood. She wondered what he might do with it.

She opened the door slowly and Sam burst right in, hurrying past her.

"Good. I didn't think you'd even let me in. We need to talk."

Amelia gritted her teeth and gave the door a mighty shove. She turned to see him laying papers out on her bed.

"I thought we had dinner plans," she let the snap of her words vibrate sharply.

"Yeah. In a moment." He'd never even looked up.

She wasn't getting the right reaction from him. He wasn't hot. He wasn't cold. He was preoccupied and that pissed her off.

Amelia walked over to the bed. "What is this?"

"Adam was killed overseas in combat."

"Not news."

He looked up from the papers, his eyes wide and bright. "It is when the family receives bereavement benefits."

"I'd forgotten all about that. My dad didn't say much about that when Mom died, but he got them."

"He would have. She was killed in combat."

Amelia nodded. "He never spoke about it though."

"Here," He said as he handed her the paperwork.

She read the information four times. "Soldiers don't make squat unless they die in combat?" She let out a long breath. "But the kids will be taken care of," she said looking up at him.

He smiled the sweetest grin she'd ever seen. "You look at that number and that's what you say?"

"Yeah. What did you expect me to say? It's very generous that the government compensates the family for their loss, but I'm not happy he died. This isn't my wish. I didn't want him in my life anymore, but what did you think? I'd be happy?"

He took the paper from her hands and set them on the bed. Then he took her hands in his.

"I've seen families pulled apart by greed. *You're* his beneficiary. You have just been handed an enormous payout. You could walk away with that and live very nicely for a very long time."

"It's not mine."

"It is, but you have a heart the size of the sun. You stayed in Oklahoma to help those women. You want to see their kids thrive. The kids of your late husband."

Amelia pulled her hands back. "I'm not some saint. Don't make me sound like that."

She turned from him, but he reached out to her again and turned her toward him. "I love you, Amelia."

Her mouth opened and she stared at him. "Oh, I didn't expect that to be how you said that."

"Can't help it. You put up this toughness and here you are changing your life to help these other women and these children that aren't yours."

"He hurt them."

"He hurt you."

"I broke his nose."

"He broke your heart."

She pursed her lips tight to fight back the tremble that was resonating in them. "My mother left me. She died for her country and my father gave us all he could. He worked hard. He volunteered at school. He sewed patches on Girl Scout uniforms. But it wasn't enough. I needed a mother. I needed *my* mother."

"Oh, Amelia." He reached for her but she backed away.

"Those girls are going to look for their father someday. Oh, they don't even remember him, but they'll need that identity. I can make them strong, Sam. I can help keep their vision of him alive, because I know that they need it. We're all tainted. He made us angry and in that anger there is hate. But he was a damn good soldier. He saved lives before he lost his. They need to know that some good lived in him and in them. Vivian and Penelope have to deal with what he left them. They have to deal with it in their own terms, but I can make them strong too." The tears were there now, but they welled in her eyes. They didn't fall.

"Who's going to keep you strong?"

The first tear fell and then the next. And soon she was sobbing like the others had.

Sam pulled her into his arms. He stroked her hair and just held her.

"Amelia," he whispered in her ear. "I want to be your strength. I want to be the one that makes you strong."

She pulled back and looked at him. "You just met me. You don't really know me."

He brushed away the tears that rolled down her cheeks. "Oh, I think I do. Give me a chance to learn more."

Amelia batted her eyes until they dried. "Don't go doing anything crazy like proposing."

"Are you sure?"

She held up a finger. "I'm sure. Don't do it. Don't even joke about it."

He was grinning with that dimple that made him so damn cute. "I said what I needed to say."

Amelia dropped her shoulders and thought about it. He had said it. "You said you loved me."

"Oh good. You were listening."

She smiled. "I told the girls you were going to tell me that tonight."

His face froze in an expression of near terror. "You told them that? You told Vivian about us?"

She bit down on her lip. "She tried to attack me." Amelia shrugged. "It was a real scene." She let the smile take over.

"I can't decide if you're making that up."

"I'm not. Not really. But she knows." Amelia moved to him. "She wasn't happy, but I think she's come along."

Sam wrapped his arms around her waist. "She won't push me down the stairs when I come to help with the house?"

"I can't promise it. But she knows I'll be kissing your wounds if she causes them." She wrapped her arms around his neck.

"So if Vivian knows what's going on, then you could move in with me…just for the time being…and get out of this place."

Amelia pressed her forehead to his. "You're a pain in the ass, you know that?"

"I know. I'm a lawyer."

"Let's talk over dinner. I'm starving."

Sam didn't drive to Oklahoma City and that pleased Amelia. Perhaps in time the rumors would begin to spread that one of Adam Monroe's widows had moved on with his lawyer. When the town actually realized there were indeed three wives of Adam Monroe. But she wasn't worried about it. As long as no one attacked Vivian or Penelope she could deal with that. She was fairly sure no one in their right mind would verbally or physically attack her.

Before they'd left the hotel she'd packed a bag. She'd go back tomorrow and check out. There was no way in hell she was actually going to move in with Sam. She was a woman who needed her space—but she needed her man close by. It didn't hurt to find out the rental Sam had told her about was literally on the next block from his house.

Over dinner they talked about the payout from the insurance. It would cover the mortgage on Vivian's house. Pay off the stupid car loan for the Mustang, which she thought they'd keep for now. And it would help get the house on Main and Pine in order so they could start their business. Once all of that was settled, Amelia wanted to get trust funds set up for the kids as well as college investments.

"What about you?" Sam asked as he lifted his after dinner cup of coffee to his lips. "What do you get?"

"So far I've gotten a new start in a new place. I'll have a new business venture. I'll even say I collected two new friends—if Vivian doesn't attack me again," she said with a smile and then leaned in over the table on her elbows. "And who'd have thought—I'd pick me up a boyfriend?"

Sam snorted a laugh. "Boyfriend? I think that sounds childish. Lover has a very nice ring to it."

Amelia sat back in her seat and clucked her tongue. "Lover? Would you like me to make you business cards?"

"Sam Jackson." He emphasized his name with his hand as though he were looking at a banner. "Lover to Amelia Monroe." He gave her that sexy grin that made her insides turn to jelly. "Make sure you include my phone number. Women will be lining up."

She shook her head. There had been enough men in her past to know this one was different. His body was sculpted differently. His hair was just a bit long and not high and tight. She couldn't get enough of him in those glasses either. Who'd have thought that just a little unbutch was her type. And to top it all off—he loved her.

Quickly she picked up her wine glass and took a big sip. He loved her and that mixed it all up.

She'd met Adam, taken him to bed, and turned around and married him. In her mind she'd written it off as an adventure to run off and get married. Spontaneity was great. But it all fell apart. The moment Adam said he loved her she had let all common sense go out the window.

Now here was Sam. She'd met him, taken him to bed, and now he said he loved her. There seemed to be a pattern even if the personality types were different.

The waiter brought the check and Sam quickly gathered it up, placed his credit card in the holder, and handed it back to him.

"Ready to go home?" he asked.

It was simple enough. It didn't mean anything, but it sent her entire body into a panic.

She'd had sex with the man—many times. She could kill him with her thumb pressed in just the right spot. Yet he had told her he loved her and that had her entire body shaking nearly uncontrollably now.

"Are you feeling okay? You're as white as a sheet," he said, his eyes wide as he looked at her.

"I am? Oh. You know, maybe I'd better go back to the hotel."

"Are you kidding me?" His voice rose. "What's going on?"

Amelia tried to catch her breath, but it wouldn't fill her lungs. "I just…"

The waiter returned with Sam's credit card. "C'mon. Let's get you some fresh air."

He pulled out her chair and took her hand. "Your hands are clammy."

There wasn't much to say. They walked outside and the air was thick and hot. It was nine-thirty at night and she broke out in a sweat.

Sam looked at her. "I'm taking you home and getting you…"

"Take me to Vivian's."

His mouth opened and then he snapped his teeth together. "What's going on?" He moved in closer to her. "You're not pregnant too are you?"

"No!" She wanted to smack him for saying that. "I just…it's just…let's go."

Sam opened the door for her and then climbed in the other side. The air whirred into the cab after he started the engine. Amelia was glad that it got cold fast. For a moment she was sure she would pass out.

Sam drove away from the restaurant. At the stoplight he looked at her. "You really want to go to Vivian's?"

She swallowed hard. "Yes. For tonight. I just…I just need to."

His fingers gripped the wheel and he turned in the opposite direction of his house and headed to Vivian's.

Chapter Nineteen

Penelope opened the door the moment they pulled into the drive. She stood there as Sam turned off the truck.

"Amelia, what's going on?" he asked as he turned toward her.

"I need a night. I just need some time."

Sam ran his hand down her hair. "Does this have anything to do with what I said to you tonight?"

"No. Yes. I mean…" She dropped her shoulders and let out a breath. "I've never been flustered over a man before."

"Flustered?"

"Yes. It's always been cut and dry. I either like him or I don't trust him. I train them or I hurt them. I can go to bed with them and wake up and go on with my life. Adam said he loved me. He didn't."

"How do you know that?"

"Look at my situation. I don't think he was capable of love. Not like you are."

Sam's hand ran over her shoulder and down her arm. "I don't understand."

"Then don't. I don't understand either. I just can't go home with you right now. I'm going to go in there and stay." She looked at the door where both Penelope and Vivian now stood. "I'm not mad. I'm actually not upset. I'm confused."

Sam let out a breath. "Okay. Can I see you tomorrow? Lunch? You can come by or I can drop by the house."

"I promise. We'll figure it out later." She moved across the console and kissed him softly. She needed to relay in that one kiss that she cared deeply for him.

When she pulled back and looked at him she felt she'd made her point.

She opened her door, stepped out, and then reached for her bag.

"I'll walk you to the..."

"No. I'm okay, Sam. Go home."

She shut the door and walked to the house. It wasn't until she was inside that she heard his tires on the gravel out front and knew he had driven away.

Penelope stood with her hand still on the door knob. "You're freaking us out. Why did you come here?"

Amelia set her bag down. "I'm sorry. I know it's late and the kids..."

"Have been in bed for nearly two hours," Vivian said. "You look like you could use a glass of wine."

Amelia nodded. "I'd like that."

She followed Vivian into the kitchen and watched as she pulled out three glasses, just as she had the first time Amelia had been there. She filled two with wine and the other with ice water.

Amelia took the glass when it was offered to her and sipped. Both Penelope and Vivian watched her from over the rims of their glasses.

When Amelia set her glass on the counter the other two lowered theirs.

"Something spooked you. What is it?" Vivian asked. "Did Sam do something? Say something?"

"Yes." She ran her hands over the legs of her pants. "He said he loved me."

Vivian shook her head and set her glass down. "You told us he was going to. What's your problem?"

"I'm scared. Adam told me he loved me too. I took that for face value and ran off and married him."

"You don't think Adam loved you?" Penelope said in a small voice.

"How can I?" Amelia asked. "I don't think he could love. Look what he did to us."

Penelope nodded and licked her lips. "Yes, but you feel love. I mean I had boys tell me they loved me all the time. But you knew they were using you. Trying to just have sex with you. But Adam, he was different."

"How so?"

Penelope shrugged. "When he said it to me we were walking, holding hands. We'd only been seeing each other a week or so, but he hadn't even tried anything with me. He stopped, gazed into my eyes, and said he loved me. It did wild things to my insides. Much like having sex with him later did. But I believe in that moment he did love me. Even if he lied to me."

Vivian and Amelia exchanged glances.

On a sigh, Vivian lifted her glass and took another sip of her wine. "I was seventeen. I met him at a party. He'd just turned eighteen. He asked me out and I thought nothing more of it than it would piss my parents off." She laughed. "We drove into Oklahoma City and went bowling with some friends. He kissed me goodnight that night and I thought I was Cinderella."

Vivian took a long drink and sat her glass down. "We went out a few more times, with friends, and then one night we separated from everyone and parked out by the lake. It was the first time anyone had ever touched me. It was amazing. We made love in the back of his pickup truck, under the stars on blankets he'd brought with him.

"I was very aware that he could get in a lot of trouble for what we'd done. I never even told my friends because I knew I loved him. I didn't want anything to happen to him. One night he reached up and cupped my cheeks in his hands and looked at me in a way he'd never looked at me before. He said he loved me and I knew—I just knew—he'd be the one. I mean, I'd already given him my virginity and taken his in return. There was nothing else to lose. I believed it."

Her lips twitched. "I believed it until after I moved back here. We'd been stationed in Germany for a year. I got homesick, came back to Parson's Gulch, he was deployed after that. When he came back it was different. I love you didn't sound the same or feel the same." She cleared her throat. "I guess I know why now."

Vivian drank down her wine until it was gone. She poured another glass. "Let's go sit in the living room. I think it'll be more comfortable."

They moved to the other room. Vivian and Penelope each tucked themselves into separate ends of the couch and Amelia sat in the oversized chair adjacent.

"What about you," Penelope said. "When did he tell you he loved you?"

Amelia couldn't believe the three of them were having this conversation and it was very civil.

"I met him at a training. It was a Wednesday. I remember that. We slept together by Thursday. He came back the following week and we eloped two weeks after that."

Vivian closed her eyes and shook her head. "It makes me ill."

"I had no idea there was anything going on that I didn't know about. I just thought it was an adventure," Amelia said softly.

"When did he say he loved you?" Penelope asked.

"The night we got married."

AMELIA

The air in the room had grown thick. It was as if they all realized love was an afterthought for Adam where Amelia was concerned.

"And yet yours was the legal marriage and you are his beneficiary," Vivian said behind her wine glass through gritted teeth.

"I should have punched him harder," Amelia said and Penelope snorted out a laugh then quickly drank from her glass. But it had started. Vivian laughed. Then Amelia laughed. Soon the tears rolled and the laugher grew louder until Ava walked out of her bedroom, eyes sleepy.

She walked over to Vivian and rested her head on her lap.

"I'm sorry honey. We were loud."

"It's okay. I like when you laugh."

Amelia felt the tightening in her chest. It was no surprise that Vivian didn't laugh often. Why would she? She'd been married to a man she'd known she loved since she was seventeen, but the years had eaten away at that. Now she had two little girls, a house that needed major upkeep, and no husband. Weave with that a lot of lies over the years and Amelia was surprised the woman could even function.

She thought about what she'd told Sam in the hotel room. She could make the girls strong. She could make Penelope and Vivian strong. What she didn't know is she could do that by experiencing everything with them. They were all hurting. They were all in the same boat, but they'd gotten there in different ways.

Just because Adam hadn't loved her like he'd loved the others didn't mean that Sam didn't.

There was a lightness in her belly now. A warmth. When Sam said he loved her she did believe it.

Vivian walked Ava back to bed and rejoined them a few minutes later. She sat back down and looked at Amelia. "You look deep in thought there," she said.

"I love Sam." The words had come softly, but quickly. There had been no thought about them. But it was there— love. The truth was on her tongue and in her heart.

Vivian laughed again, picked up her glass, and raised it in toast. "Good."

Amelia looked at both of them smiling at her. But she was, herself, too stunned to smile. "I do. I just realized *that's* what I've been feeling."

"Why are you here then?"

"Because I didn't know what to do with that." She placed her hand on her chest because her heart was racing so fast. "I love him."

"Do you need a ride over to his place?" Vivian asked.

"No. I think I'll wait," Amelia said sipping from her glass.

She'd wait until the moment was exactly right to tell him how she felt. Spontaneity hadn't worked for her in the past. Overthinking never did her much good either. There had to be some middle ground and when she found it she'd tell Sam what she'd learned about herself. But for tonight she'd sip wine with her new friends and sleep on Vivian's couch.

Chapter Twenty

The sun was bright as it flooded through the windows in Vivian's living room. Amelia covered her eyes with her arm and then heard the small giggles.

She turned to see Ava and Emma sitting in the chair across from her, both bundled in the same blanket, watching her.

"What are you girls doing?" she asked. Her voice full of sleep and gruff.

"You snore." Ava said innocently, which warranted a jab from her sister. "She does. And she talks."

Even Amelia had to laugh at that. She sat up and rubbed the sleep from her eyes.

"I snore and talk, huh? Did I say something funny?"

The girls exchanged looks. Emma looked perplexed as she obviously thought about what Amelia had said.

The look had Amelia sitting up and looking at her. "Honey, what did I say?"

"You were mad. You were mad at someone about a baby." She looked at her sister. "You kept saying Adam. Like our daddy's name."

Amelia felt the blood drain from her head and it was only made worse when she heard a gasp from behind her.

"Girls, you go get your breakfast. Go." Vivian's voice was loud and demanding.

The girls scrambled off the chair and ran to the kitchen.

Amelia rested her face in her hands. "Oh, God. Oh, God."

"Yeah, oh, God." Vivian plopped down next to her on the couch. "Crap."

"I didn't mean…I wouldn't have…oh, God!"

They sat there for a moment in silence.

"I have to tell them," Vivian finally said. "They deserve the truth."

"Vivian, I'm so sorry. I didn't…"

Vivian turned to her with her eyes fixed and hard. "You're not the kind of woman who is sorry for anything, so shut up. Obviously it's on your conscience."

"Of course it is. Especially now that I know what you went through when Ava was born. I can't help but feel responsible."

"Unless you knew what I was going through while you were sleeping with my husband then you're not at fault." Her voice rose in tone and volume, but she tightened her eyes and rolled her shoulders as if to reel herself back in. "It's not your fault."

"What are you two doing?" Penelope stood in the doorway. "The girls are in here whispering. You're out here yelling."

Vivian shook her head and looked at Amelia. "You see what he did, don't you? He married us another wife—a mother."

Amelia laughed but Penelope stomped her foot on the ground. "What's going on?" The tears were already there and Vivian only shook her head before she stood and went to her. She took her by the arms and led her to the couch.

"Sit."

"I don't want to sit. I want to know…"

"Sit."

Penelope sat down where Vivian had sat and Vivian paced.

"They're my girls. I'll tell them." She ran her hands through her dark hair. "I'll tell them. You go get ready for work," she said to Penelope. "And you, get up and get a shower," she said to Amelia.

Amelia stood and took Penelope's hand to help her to her feet. "C'mon. Mom is mad. We'd better go to our rooms."

"What's going on?"

Amelia let out a long breath as Vivian went back to the kitchen. "She's going to tell them about their dad and us." She went against all personal space protocols and laid her hand on Penelope's stomach. "And about the baby."

The tears were back—again and Penelope shook her hands as if they were wet and that would stop the tears. "They're going to hate me. They're going to hate my baby."

"They aren't haters. They'll need to adjust. But they'll love the baby." She put her hands on Penelope's shoulders. "C'mon. You need to get ready for work and I need a ride into town. My truck is still at the hotel."

Penelope stopped and turned to her. "You really love him?"

Amelia gave some thought to her astonished realization from the night before. "I do. Is that crazy?"

"I think it's lovely."

"I just met him."

"Just because it follows a similar time frame of your last relationship doesn't mean it's bad."

Amelia laughed. "I guess when I think about it I've been with Sam longer than I had been with Adam before I married him."

"I think it's very sweet."

"I just think it's nice I have someone who can share in the mistake with me. I never should have trusted him and married him."

Penelope shook her head. "It's not a mistake. It was a path." She looked Amelia in the eye. "Fate does some crazy things when it has too. Without Adam you wouldn't have Sam. Vivian needed friends to bond with and here we are."

"What about you?"

Penelope took a deep breath and let it out as she placed her hands on her stomach. "I might not have Adam, but I have my baby. *My* baby. What a gift."

"You have us too you know. You're not alone."

"I consider that a bonus."

In a pair of Victoria Secret PINK sweatpants and a fitted T-shirt Amelia borrowed from Penelope, she walked out into the living room after her shower.

Her hair was still damp and her mouth only freshened by a swish of SCOPE.

Vivian sat on the couch, her head rested against the back of it. Amelia could hear the girls playing outside.

Penelope walked from the kitchen with two mugs of coffee. She looked in Amelia's direction.

"I didn't grab one for you. Do you want one?"

"I'm fine." She walked around the couch and looked at Vivian. "Are you okay?"

Vivian's eyes were closed and her cheeks tear stained. "That was as bad as telling them their daddy had died."

Amelia sat down in the chair across from her. "How did they take it?"

Vivian raised her head. "Just as well as they took the news of his death."

"So they're upset?" Amelia asked.

Penelope sat down in the other chair which faced the couch. Her hands were clasped tightly in her lap.

Vivian ran her hands through her hair. "No, they weren't upset. That's the whole thing. When I told them he died they consoled me. They didn't know him. Ava didn't know him at all. He'd only been around a few times."

That stabbed at Amelia. Knowing that if he was with Ava he'd lied to her to be there.

"Emma didn't remember him too much. So to tell them that their daddy was," she contemplated her words, "having another baby, they just took it in stride."

"They hugged me," Penelope said. "They touched my stomach and hugged me. I didn't think they'd do that." Her voice shook.

"So they're okay?" Amelia asked.

"Too okay," Vivian answered. "They should have been a little bit upset. They should have cared a little. But now they're all excited to have a little sister."

"Or brother," Penelope said softly.

"Or brother," Vivian said as she rolled her head back again and let out a long breath. "God, who thought this would be the way everything would happen. I trusted him. I loved him. He gave me my girls and then I have to tell them about his lies and deceptions."

Amelia heard Penelope sniff back tears. She understood the feelings. She too now felt like a lie and a deception.

Penelope had dropped Amelia by the hotel on her way to work. She changed her clothes as she was much too old, she thought, to wear Penelope's clothes.

Amelia pulled her hair up into a ponytail and brushed her teeth. Then, she looked around the small room. It was silly to keep paying for the space.

She sat down on the bed and clasped her hands in her lap. In a few weeks she could have the townhouse. Penelope could stay with Vivian if she wanted or she could certainly move in with her.

She hated feeling petty about wanting Penelope to choose one or the other of them. And worse, she wanted her to choose her.

Blowing out a breath she looked around again. It was time to check out.

If she knew Sam Jackson, the man who had said he loved her and she'd admitted she loved too, then he'd still offer to let her stay with him.

But she'd let him come to her. He said he'd come by the house later. She'd let him.

Amelia went about clearing up the room and packing her belongings. It was time to move on. She was ready to leave behind the life as Adam Monroe's wife. It was time to make a home in Parson's Gulch, embrace the love she had with Sam Jackson, and start a business with the women she had forced into her life—and whom she'd embraced as well.

~*~

Sam stopped off at the hardware store before heading to the house on Main and Pine. Amelia hadn't stopped by the office so he assumed that meant he needed to stop by the house.

As promised, he'd fix the steps. Most of his day had been spent researching what needed to be done. He was feeling fairly confident. Besides, he had enough handy friends if he needed them. He could call in one or two—or ten of them.

The moment he pulled up in front of the house, he saw the baskets of flowers he'd brought hanging on the porch. Amelia stood at the base to the steps of the porch. She was hovering over the bush he'd brought with a shovel.

As he climbed out of the truck he called up to her. "Do you need some help with that?"

"You're timing is impeccable. I'm done."

"Good," he said and laughed.

She looks okay, he thought. Penelope had said she was fine that morning, but he hadn't dug for too much information. He didn't want to use Penelope like that.

But Amelia was going to have to explain to him what went wrong last night. He thought everything was fine and then she'd just flipped out. Something had set that off and he needed to know what that was.

Sam lowered the tailgate on his truck and began pulling the supplies to the end of the bed. Amelia set her shovel by the pillar to the porch and walked toward him.

"What's all this?" she asked as she neared him.

"Came to start on those stairs."

"Are you sure you didn't just come to see if I'd throw that shovel at you?"

He gave her a chuckle. "Thought crossed my mind I suppose."

Amelia moved in toward him and he opened so she could. She rested her hands on his hips and he brushed a piece of her hair from her forehead.

"I'm sorry about last night. I really am."

"You don't have to be."

"But I am. You telling me you loved me shook me up a little bit. Then when you said we should go home, I panicked."

"You've stayed at my place before."

"But not when it was *us* going *home*. I've gone to your house before. But that wasn't what you meant."

Sam cupped her face. "No. It wasn't what I meant."

"I calmed down once I settled in at Vivian's. I just had to sort it all out."

"And what did you come up with?"

Amelia dropped her shoulders and looked up into his eyes. "I checked out of the hotel today."

"Good. That was good money being wasted."

"It was." She raised her arms and linked them around his neck. "I figured that it wouldn't be a big deal to stay with you until the townhouse is available to rent."

"That's good too," he said wrapping his arms around her waist.

"I found out a lot of things last night." She wound her fingers up into his hair. "Ava and Emma say I snore and I talk in my sleep."

"No comment."

"Hmmm," she grunted. "I guess I speak very clearly." She looked down at his chest and took a moment before looking back up at him. "I somehow said something about a baby in a fight with Adam."

Sam pulled back just enough to look at her. "You said that?"

She nodded. "Vivian had to tell the girls."

"Oh," he let it ride on a sigh. "What did they say?"

"They're excited to have a baby sister."

"Or brother."

She laughed easily. "They don't really know Adam. This is just another thing to happen to them."

"I get that. I'm glad it got out in the open. Did you tell them about the life insurance policy?"

Amelia looked at him. Her face had gone puzzled. "I forgot all about it."

"You did?"

"Yes, I'd had another epiphany and didn't think about it I guess."

"And what was that?"

"First of all that I'm still a girl and able to have all those confused girlie feelings."

"Right. We established you were just that and allowed to have them."

She gave him a nudge. "With these two women in my life I seem to be embracing that...that...*sisterly* factor I guess. The kind where you can let those emotions play out in front of someone to get resolve."

"And what was the resolve?"

She pressed a kiss to his lips and then sunk into it. "I realized I loved you too."

He pulled her closer and held her there. "I never thought you'd get to that realization."

"I was avoiding it."

"Well, I'm glad that's over." He kissed her again, this time deeper, fuller.

When he stepped back he noticed Penelope and Vivian on the porch watching with smiles before they both hurried back into the house.

"I guess they're okay with us?"

"I think they are. She looked up toward the house. I genuinely think they are."

Sam smoothed a hand over her ponytail. "Why don't we let this wait a bit and go in and tell them about the policy. They need to know that they have some breathing room when it comes to the estate."

She nodded and he took her hand and headed into the house.

Chapter Twenty-One

Vivian and Penelope were in the dining room scraping old wallpaper off of the walls when Sam and Amelia walked in. There was some Blake Shelton blaring from an iPod and that seemed to ease Amelia's nerves.

"Do you girls have a moment to talk business?" Sam asked.

Both women looked up with grins spread over their faces.

"Really, Sam, you don't have to discuss the birds and the bees with us. We know what happens after you kiss a woman like that. After all, we're the ones who have been knocked up."

Vivian and Penelope giggled and Sam's face had gone red.

"What?" He choked.

"Nothing," Amelia interrupted. "Don't listen to these childish girls." She shot him a smile.

"I get it. This is an inside joke. The three of you have bonded enough to have inside jokes."

They all exchanged glances. "I guess we have," Vivian said standing and stretching her back. "Who'd have thought? Because I really had wanted to kick Amelia's ass."

"It humors her that she tried." Amelia crossed her arms over her chest.

"Maybe someday you'll be the one on your ass," Vivian shot back.

"Don't give up on your training." Amelia let the remark hang. "But honestly," she gave them a serious tone. "Sam has some news to share with us."

Vivian gave a somber look to Penelope and then shifted it to Sam. "Is everything okay? God, please don't tell me there is more bad news. Don't tell me he has four or five wives. Or he had gambling debt that he owes the mafia."

Sam shook his head. "Do you have some iced tea in the fridge?"

Penelope nodded. "I just put a new batch in there."

"Let's sit down and have some tea. I'll tell you what I know."

Penelope poured iced tea into plastic cups and Amelia found some buckets to set in the kitchen for chairs.

Sam had run out to his truck to grab the paperwork he'd shown to Amelia the night before.

They all stopped what they were doing as he walked into the kitchen.

"You girls are too high strung and serious," he said setting the papers on the table. "Not everything is always bad news."

"It is when Adam Monroe's name is attached," Vivian said through gritted teeth.

"Well then you can thank your United States armed services for this reprieve." He handed her the envelope.

Vivian pulled the papers out and looked them over. Her eyes shifted as she read the words.

She thumbed through the documents and went back to read the first page again.

"Oh, what is it?" Penelope asked nearly frantic.

"This is the life insurance policy from the Army. Since Adam was killed overseas in combat…well look." She handed Penelope the paper with the payout number on it and Penelope's eyes grew wide.

"Oh…"

"You girls can pay off his debts and fix up this house for your business. Vivian, there should be enough to pay off the mortgage on your home."

Vivian placed her hand on her chest. "That would take a load off of my mind."

Amelia stood and moved to the table. "We can clear the auto loan and keep the car for now. We should hold on to it and sell it when we need more capital."

"That's a good idea," Vivian agreed.

"What do we do with the rest of it?" Penelope asked.

Sam exchanged looks with Amelia and she gave him a nod.

"I've been working on that today. Amelia would like to set up trust funds and college accounts for Adam's three children."

"Why?" Vivian was quick to shoot out the question. "Why would you do that?" Vivian pushed back from the table, her voice accusing.

"They are the real victims in this," Amelia said. "They lost their father."

"He wasn't much of one and you know that."

"Well, then he pays for that."

"This leaves you with nothing. Why do I feel like I'm missing something?" Vivian turned fully to face Amelia. "You gave up your home in Georgia. You had sex with the lawyer," Vivian said and Amelia saw Sam's cheeks deepen in color. "Now you're going to pay off the bills and give our kids all the money left over?"

"I don't see what you're missing."

"Who does that? Who just steps in and makes sure everyone is taken care of and doesn't ask for something of her own?"

"Me," Amelia said calmly because it was truth.

"I...I just..." Vivian blew out a breath. "Thank you."

Penelope had a different approach. She moved to Amelia and gave her a hug.

It wasn't just a quick hug though. She held her until Amelia patted her back and she stepped back. "This is very generous of you." Penelope placed her hands on the slight—very slight—rise of her stomach.

"It's not generous of me at all. He died for this—for us. I don't like being the only one in that will that was named. I don't like that out of three marriages I'm the only legal heir to anything. Those girls," she pointed to the other room where Ava and Emma sat watching a movie on an iPad. "And your baby," she pointed to Penelope. "Deserve everything. I know what it is to have lost a parent in combat. I know what part of you is hollowed out and never filled. They don't deserve that." She sucked in a breath before she continued.

"They deserve to have a roof over their heads and a fine education. Adam's death will provided that. Not the best way for him to take care of them, but it's something."

"And you don't want anything in return?" Vivian, still with an edge to her voice, asked.

Amelia dropped her shoulders and gave it some thought. "Fine. What I want when this house is done and your house is paid off and all the accounts have been set up," she took a breath out of frustration. "What I want is space in the basement for a training facility. A heavy bag. Some mats. Some weights. It'll save me on a gym membership. How's that?"

"Totally selfish," Vivian said and Amelia stepped forward to shake her if she had to before Vivian broke into laughter. "I'm kidding. God, lighten up."

Penelope laughed and then Sam did too.

"Amelia, you have to learn not to take everything so seriously," Vivian humored herself as she put the papers back in the envelope Sam had brought in. And then she turned to her. "But again, thank you. Your compassion speaks levels about your character."

After a few solid hours of work on the house, Sam cleaned up his mess and started for his truck. Amelia sat on the front porch with a glass of iced tea.

"Where are the others?"

"They left a little while ago. The girls needed dinner and they have a routine."

Sam gave her a nod. "I sometimes forget what it takes when you have children to think about."

Amelia looked down into her glass. "Vivian is a good mother. She really is."

"I see that."

"And even though sometimes I wonder what kind of brains rattle in Penelope's head, I think she'll be a good mother too."

"I see that too just by the way she is with Vivian's girls."

"I'm not sure I'd be a good mother. I don't have the first idea of how it all works. I mean my mother shouted out commands. My mother wasn't like Vivian who embraces her daughters."

Sam sat down next to her and rested his hand on her back. He felt her tense, but he didn't pull back.

"Don't get me wrong. I know my mother loved me. I know that she loved all of us. But her career was just more important."

"But you had your father. He taught you compassion and love."

She smiled. "Yes he did."

"I think when the time comes you'll be okay." He took her hand in his and gave it a squeeze.

"I'd never considered having kids. It wasn't something Adam and I ever discussed at all." She rested her head on his shoulder. "But I think about it with you."

He couldn't help it. Pride swelled in his chest. "That's a big step for you."

"It is. Especially since I've only really known you a few weeks."

"We have a long time to get to know each other. It doesn't stop the fact that I already know I want to spend the rest of my life with you."

She held up a finger to him.

"I'm not proposing. I know better."

Amelia gave him a nod. "I think I'm ready to go home now, though. With you."

Sam lifted his hand and caressed her cheek. "I'm ready for that too. And I know you plan to make that temporary. But I'm here to tell you I'm going to try and talk you out of that."

He pulled her in until their lips met. As far as he was concerned he never wanted her living in another place again.

~*~

The air was too hot outside to open a window. Sam made sure the air conditioner was set comfortably and he turned on the ceiling fan as well.

Amelia lay in his bed. Right where she belonged, he thought. The tank top she wore hugged her firm, toned body. Her arm was up over her head and dark hair fanned out over the pillow. She was a sight of beauty.

Even though the girls had told her she snored he'd never bring it up himself. It was—endearing.

She'd said she was going to wait for him, but obviously the past week of working on the house and teaching had caught up to her. Now she slept.

Sam turned off the light and walked to the other side of the bed. He pulled off his T-shirt and stretched his arms and back. Working on those stairs was quite a chore.

He folded back the sheet and climbed in next to Amelia. She stirred slightly as he got situated. He leaned over to kiss her goodnight, but was met with a stiff hand to the chest which had him rolling onto his back and gasping for air.

"Oh, God!" She bolted up. "I'm sorry. You startled me."

Quickly, Amelia turned on the bedside lamp and looked at him with his hand on his chest.

"Oh, look at the bruise on you. I hit you there didn't I?"

"Yep," he was sucking in air weakly.

The bruise from the attic stair incident the day before was prominently displayed on his chest nearly reaching from one armpit to the other. He'd worked through the discomfort when he'd been working at the house, but this—this took the cake.

Amelia moved his hands and examined the bruise. "We need to remember to fix the attic entry before this happens to someone else."

"We'll add that to the list of everything," he winced as he readjusted in the bed.

"Did it hurt all day?"

"Just when I thought about it."

Amelia rolled to her side, propped herself up next to him. Gently—ever so gently—she pressed her lips to the injured skin.

"Does that hurt?"

"No."

She pressed another kiss to it. "That?"

"No." His responses were becoming weaker and breathier.

She'd kiss and ask again. Soon his answer was not coming from his mouth, but from a significant member of his body.

Amelia stripped off her tank top and pulled off the shorts she'd worn to bed.

"Maybe I can make up for the attic stairs and hitting you too."

"Okay. I'll let you try."

She straddled him, leaning over him careful not to press her weight to him.

Her hair fell around them like a private curtain and she moved her mouth against his.

"You'll feel better soon, I promise."

Chapter Twenty-Two

As summer gave into the last few days before fall the heat still sweltered. Progress on the old house was made a little at a time, usually early in the morning and late at night.

The flowers which Sam had brought were bright and full. The bush seemed happy in its little home by the steps.

During the day, Vivian worked on acquiring all the right licenses and learning about the business they were going into. She understood the growth and learning curve of young children, but the business end of child care was a whole different ballgame.

Penelope kept herself cool in the office of Lawyer Sam Jackson. Sam made sure there was something under the desk for her to put her feet up. He had stocked the small refrigerator with waters and healthy snacks. And it was no longer her job to get them lunch. He'd seen to that too.

Amelia, who had purchased a personal cooler to be worn around her neck, worked inside the house alone with her music every day until the others got there. A few days a week, they worked until late at night with the girls falling asleep on a pile of small pillows Penelope had brought for them. Other nights they all went home to relax and Amelia would teach. Once in a while she convinced the others to join her. Weekends—those were for hard, sweaty labor.

Amelia's project at the moment was the larger bedroom upstairs. She wanted to make it something very special for Penelope. When the baby came, Amelia wanted Penelope to have a place. Something they could call their own. So, with that, she'd been fixing up the bathroom and patching the walls. A few more weeks and it would be done. But she didn't want Penelope to live there until the entire house was done. The fumes and dust wouldn't be good on her.

It was optimistic, she knew, but she wanted the house done by the beginning of November. They'd miss the beginning of the school year and those new enrollments. But that was okay. They'd be ready for the following year and by then they'd have more experience. And by "they" she meant Vivian and Penelope. She surely didn't have any talent in that area and she wasn't going to pretend she did. The thought had crossed her mind that when the house was done perhaps she'd take the attic and convert it into an office.

If, and only if they'd taken her seriously, she'd put a training facility in the basement and she could teach some private classes there. The thought actually thrilled her.

It was nearly five-thirty when Amelia heard a car pull up in front of the house. Penelope slowly moved out of her car.

Her body had changed as she moved through her second trimester. Vivian had told her at the beginning of August that she'd popped. The term seemed to have thrilled Penelope, but baffled Amelia. She saw it now, though. Penelope waddled from the ever growing size of her belly. She was nearly half way there—Adam's last baby would be born soon. That would be another rush of feelings for another day, Amelia thought.

She finished the task at hand and closed the door to the bedroom before walking down the new steps Sam had created.

Penelope opened the door and slowly walked in.

"You look beat," Amelia said.

"I am. My hands are swollen. My ankles are swollen. I'm about three hundred degrees in these clothes and all I want is a cool bath."

"Then why are you here?"

"Because everyone will be here soon and this is what we do for now. We have to get this place ready."

Amelia noted that Penelope had taken off her normal shoes and slipped into a pair of ugly Crocs. At least she wouldn't get something stuck in her foot and her ankles could have some room.

"I have bottles of water in the fridge. I'll get you one. You come in the kitchen and sit down and put your feet up."

Penelope nodded and followed her to the back of the house.

"Sam will be by soon, he said. He was going to pick up something for dinner. He said he had a hankering for a slab of meat on the grill."

Amelia laughed easily as she pulled the bottle of water out of the refrigerator for Penelope.

"I think it's too hot to work tonight. Maybe we should all go home and get some rest."

Penelope nodded and Amelia could see the fatigue in her eyes. "There's a storm brewing too. You can see it forming. Maybe we'll get some rain and it'll cool this heat down."

"I'd be okay with that." Amelia pulled out another bottle of water and opened it. "I guess I should text Sam and Vivian and tell them just to head home."

Penelope looked around the ugly kitchen. "The house is looking really good. I guess this gets done last, huh?"

"Makes sense. It's the most updated part of the house at this point. So, it might be ugly, but it's functional."

Penelope nodded, sipped her water, and looked back up at Amelia. "I have a doctor appointment next week. I'll be almost through my five months." She licked her lips in consideration. "I'm going to have an ultrasound. I think I'll find out the sex of the baby."

"Is that an accurate thing? They can tell you that?"

"Yes. I've been reading up on it. Vivian bought me a book."

There was that pang of girlie jealousy she hated so much creeping into her gut. She wished it away—willed it gone.

"That's very nice."

"I don't know if you're too busy with the house or teaching, but I'd like you and Vivian to be there."

Now the jealousy that had nearly made her nauseous had spun into guilt and pride and love—yes love. Love for a friend. Penelope had trusted her since the moment they'd met. Now she was asking her to be part of something so special that Amelia thought she just might cry.

"Are you sure you want me there? This is your thing. I don't..."

"It's all of us. Adam isn't going to be there—ever."

"In spirit I suppose."

Penelope shook her head. "You know when someone dies and you can feel them? I have that with my grandmother. I often feel like she's with me. Watching out for me. I've never felt that with Adam."

Amelia did know what she was talking about and she had to agree. She'd never felt it with him either.

"If you're too busy, or it's too awkward I'd understand. I just thought I'd..."

"I'd love to come. It means a lot that you'd want me there."

Penelope smiled now and Amelia's chest tightened. She didn't think it would be possible to love again. Sam had proven her wrong. She'd fallen in love with him so hard her head still spun. But to fall in love with a friend—that was different. Never would she have thought that when Sam Jackson, attorney, told her that there was one more Mrs.

Monroe than she'd already known about, she'd love that woman like a sister when she very clearly could have been the enemy.

Chapter Twenty-Three

Amelia drove home with tiny beads of rain on the windshield. The sky had quickly been consumed by gray. The temperature hadn't dipped much with the rain. Lightning illuminated the sky line.

Oklahoma was a magnet for a good storm. And though severe storms weren't unheard of at the end of the summer, she'd have worried more if it were May.

Amelia had a great appreciation for a good storm. It was like temper brewing and that was something she understood very well.

When she was a young girl and there was thunder her friends would say it was angels bowling. She, however, thought of it as gun fire—her mother's gunfire.

It made her feel as if her mother were protecting her, no matter where in the world she was. She felt her, just as Penelope felt her grandmother, but neither of them felt Adam.

When lightning would streak the sky with its brilliance Amelia actually smiled. She imagined fairies dancing with traces of light. Even as an adult she could refocus her mind to keep her calm. It was a good thing. This year her calm had been tested.

She pulled up in front of the townhouse she now shared with Sam. She smiled wide. The other townhouse had been available for weeks, she knew that. But Sam hadn't mentioned it and she'd grown so comfortable that she didn't want to leave.

She locked the door to her truck as a thunderous bolt of lightning crashed through the sky and the ground shook with the reply.

The air was full of electricity and the hair on the back of her neck stood on end.

She hurried up the steps and as she opened the front door a gust of wind blew it out of her hand sending it back and through the wall.

Sam hurried out of the kitchen, a huge knife in his hand and an apron with the depiction of Superman's body covering his own.

"Jesus, are you okay?"

Amelia pushed the door shut and went about assessing the damage where the doorknob had punched through the drywall.

"I'm fine, but the wall didn't fare as well."

Sam walked to her, the knife still gripped in his hand. "Flesh wound."

"Good thing we're becoming experts on home improvement."

He laughed and she examined him with the knife and the apron.

"What are you doing in there?"

"Dinner. Steaks. Potatoes. Salad."

She gave the apron a tug. "What's with this?"

"My sister's humor. Cute huh?"

She pressed her lips together. "I certainly like the Clark Kent look. The Superman is equally as interesting."

Amelia moved in and laid her lips to his.

"We could hold off on dinner," he said, his voice deep and resonating with a sexy vibration that had her skin tingle.

"As appealing as that is," she swallowed hard trying to pull herself back into the moment. "Perhaps you should put the weapon down."

Sam laughed. "Well if I have to go in there and set the knife down we'd better just eat. Especially since you came home early and if I don't get this cooked soon I'll be doing it in a storm."

Another roll of thunder shook the house. "You'd better take an umbrella out there with you. I'll help you with that salad."

Amelia thought she'd never tire of cooking with Sam in the kitchen. Nor would she ever want to sleep in another bed. The storm had settled but the air was still thick. She'd opened the window before she climbed into bed and Sam wrapped his arm around her.

He lingered a kiss on her neck. "This bed never was as comfortable as it has been for the past few weeks."

"Oh, yeah?" She said with her voice airy and soft.

"It needed a woman in it. It needed you."

She rolled to face him. His arm remained around her. "I was just thinking how I can't imagine ever sleeping anywhere else."

His eyes were closed, but he smiled a smile which squeezed at her heart. "That townhouse has been vacant for weeks," he said.

She bit down on her lip. "It has, huh? I suppose I should think about getting out of here."

Sam's arm pulled her in tighter to him, his eyes still closed. "Rent is cheaper here."

"Food is better here too. In my condo I used to only eat over the sink."

Sam nuzzled his nose against hers as the curtains began to blow in the breeze. "So did I until you came along."

"Maybe I'd better stay a while longer then. I mean I'd hate for you to go back to your old ways," she rubbed her lips against his.

"I don't run."

Amelia pulled back from him and studied the humor on his face. "What does that mean?"

He opened his eyes slightly. "Don't expect me to get up and go running with you. I don't run."

"I don't do yoga."

"Okay, then we're set. You're staying—forever."

She watched him, but he remained calm and casual, but her body had tensed. Had he noticed? Was he just making small talk?

Why was she worrying about it? Hadn't she said to herself that she didn't want to go anywhere else?

Sam rolled her to her back and looked down at her. "I just said, we're set and you're staying forever."

"I heard you. I'm wrapping my head around that. It's exactly what I want."

"That's what I wanted to hear." He reached his hand under her pillow.

"What are you doing?"

"Looking for this," he said as he pulled out a ring and held it up in the dim light.

Amelia tried to sit up, but he was on top of her. Okay, she wasn't trying hard enough. It wouldn't take but the slightest bit of a shove upward to send him flying. But she looked at the shimmering object he held between his fingers which caught the moonlight.

"Sam, what is that? What are you doing?"

"I bought you a gift."

"That's a ring."

She could see the white of his teeth as he smiled. "You're right. It is."

"Why? Why do you have that?"

"I wanted you to wear it."

"I said not to propose. I said I loved you, but you said you wouldn't propose."

"I don't think I did."

Now she moved. She locked her legs tightly around him and rolled him onto his back.

He let out a grunt. "What? You don't like it?"

"I don't want to like it."

"That wasn't my question."

She rose up and looked down at him pulling the ring from his hand. "You bought me a ring and want to know if I like it?"

"And I want to know if you'll stay forever."

"That's two questions."

"Yes, but I didn't propose."

He was grinning. Damn it—he was grinning.

"You want to marry me?"

Sam sat up to meet her and wrapped his arms around her. His hands pressed against her back and his breath skimmed her skin as he brushed a kiss against her neck.

"You drive a hard bargain, but I'll marry you."

"What?"

"You just asked if I wanted to marry you. I do." He kissed her again as the wind blew through the room and the curtains snapped. "You just proposed to me."

"Sam! You…you…tricked me."

"Oh, I don't think so. Don't you want me to marry you?"

"Yes I want to marry you…"

"Good. Then this is settled—again." He took the ring from the hand where she gripped it and slid it on her finger. "Much better."

She was fuming. She felt it. It was about to burst out of her just like the roll of thunder outside the window. But the ring caught the moonlight. It shimmered.

Amelia looked down at Sam who, bright eyed, smiled at her. "It looks nice on you."

"Sam…"

"Now don't go crying."

It wasn't the emotion she thought would burst through, but it was. Tears rolled down her cheeks. "You didn't propose."

"Nope, you did."

Now a laugh broke through as the curtains blew harder in the window. "I did."

"Yes, you did."

"You're going to marry me. And not because it's just something to do. You love me."

"Oh, honey, I do love you."

"Well then," she lowered him to the bed and moved her mouth against his. "I'm glad you agreed to marry me."

Sam pulled her closer and opened his mouth to her kiss. His tongue moved to dance with hers and her breath began to grow thick like the air in the room.

The curtains slapped into the room and against the wind. Hail began pelting the house with an abusive force. Amelia sat up and moved off the bed.

As she reached the windows the tornado warning sirens in town began to blare.

She looked toward Sam who jumped from the bed, grabbed her hand, and his cell phone. He hit the flashlight on the phone and pulled her though the hall, down the stairs, and to the basement.

Chapter Twenty-Four

Sam pushed through the boxes he stored in the basement and pulled Amelia under the staircase.

"Get down! Cover your head!" he yelled over the freight train sound as he crouched down next to her and covered her with his body.

He could hear the wind pick up and he was fairly sure he could hear the patio chairs being thrown against the outside of the house.

Amelia covered her ears and Sam kept his body atop of hers.

The noise was horrific, but Sam knew they weren't in the midst of the major part of the tornado. He'd been through more warnings, sirens, and actual tornados than he'd like to count.

He could smell the upturned earth just outside, but the air suddenly stilled.

Sam eased off of Amelia slightly.

"Is it over?" she asked.

He could feel her tremble beneath him. "Sounds like it, but we sit here for a few more minutes."

She nodded raising her head slowly. Sam sat back on his heels and listened. The air had gone still and the night was quiet and dark. There were no sounds in the house.

"Power's off," he said in a whisper.

"Did it touch down?" Amelia sat back on her heels.

"I don't know." He stood and held his hand out to her. "Let's go upstairs and see if we can see anything."

As they crested the stairs he couldn't see any immediate damage. He walked slowly toward the back door and confirmed that the grill was across the yard and the furniture had been thrown. That, he thought, was pretty lucky.

He could see flashlights in the neighborhood as people began to move about assessing damage.

"Do you have your phone?" he asked.

She looked around. "I set it on the kitchen table." She walked across the dark room, illuminated only by his cellphone light. "I have it."

"Check the news channel feeds. See what it says."

Amelia pulled up her phone's browser and typed in the local news channel.

The warnings, the weather—the touchdown.

"It did. It touched down." She scanned the story. "It stayed out of town, but touched down on the northwest side of Parson's Gulch."

Her head rose and he knew that moment that they were thinking the same thing.

"Call. Get them on the phone. Get your shoes. We're heading over there," he said, heading to slip on his shoes and get his car keys.

Amelia jumped into Sam's truck and pushed the contact button for Penelope for the third time. And for the third time it went to voice mail just as Vivian's had done the four times earlier.

Sam backed out of the driveway and started toward Vivian's.

There were downed power lines and trees. A few houses had blown out windows, but there didn't seem to be a path of where the tornado traveled. At least in the headlights of Sam's truck they couldn't see anything—that was until they were within a mile of Vivian's house.

Trees were uprooted. Cars had been tossed. The church on the corner was missing part of its roof.

Amelia's heart began to pound in her chest. "Oh, God. Hurry. Hurry."

"I'll get there. Just keep trying them."

The air was thick and smelled of mud. Amelia tried to suck in as much as she could with her shirt pressed to her nose.

As Sam turned down Vivian's street he slowed. "I don't think it touched down here, but it was close."

Debris covered the street and he had to stop the truck. "We have to go on foot."

He pulled a Maglite flashlight out from under his seat. He stepped out of his truck. Amelia followed.

They walked down the dark street. There was a car on its side. Every trash can and lawn chair had been blown out of the yards.

As they reached Vivian's corner, Amelia gripped Sam's arm. "Oh, God!" She took off running and he kept up right behind her. The light from his flashlight and the slightest sliver of the moon shined down to illuminate the house.

A tree had collapsed into the side of it. Amelia knew that it was the kitchen and living room which were damaged and all she could hope for was that if they were in that house they were in the bedroom.

"Vivian! Penelope! Emma! Ava!" She screamed as she made it to the front of the house and up to the door. "It's locked! It's locked!" She turned to Sam. "Go around back."

They carefully made it around the house yelling for the four of them with no response.

Amelia had nerves of steel, but when she saw the sliding back door smashed in she felt sick. "We have to get in there."

"We will," Sam said as he looked around the yard with his flashlight. He shined it against the fence. "There's a chair. Hold this." He handed her the flashlight and she shined it so he could get through the yard.

"Hurry."

She yelled for them again. But still there was no answer.

Sam hurried back with the chair. "Move. Cover your eyes."

He took the chair and gave it a mighty swing through the glass. Shards flew into the house and the bigger pieces that were already broken crashed to the ground.

Sam took his foot and kicked in the rest so they could climb through.

When they were both in the house he shined the light around. "Are they even home?"

"It's ten o'clock at night. They have to be home." She felt her way through the dining room. The furniture was thrown through the house as if someone had ransacked the place. Pieces of the ceiling hung in the kitchen, but she knew they hadn't been in there.

"Vivian! Penelope!" She headed down the hall. "All of the bedroom doors are open. The beds are made."

Sam moved to the window. "Penelope's car is outside. Against the neighbor's."

Amelia yelled again and this time when she did her phone rang in her hand.

"Vivian! Where are you? Are you hurt? Where are the girls and Penelope?"

"Jesus, Amelia. We're fine. We're at the old house. We were working on it."

"You're okay? God," she said to Sam. "They're okay."

"We were in the storm shelter. It took us a while to get out with all the debris. My phone wouldn't work down there."

"But you're all okay?" She let out a breath, but her heart still pounded in her chest.

"Yes. Are you and Sam okay?"

Amelia reached for Sam and took his hand. She gave it a squeeze as she looked around. "We're fine. We're at your house."

"My house?"

"It touched down out here."

"Oh, no," her voice had trailed off on the sigh. "The house? Do I even want to know?"

Amelia looked at the other end of the house where the large tree was balanced. "The tree out front. It crashed into the house."

"Oh! Oh!" She could hear the tears in Vivian's voice.

"Penelope's car is damaged too."

She heard her relay the message and Penelope began to sob.

"You're safe. That's all that matters." Sam wrapped his arm around Amelia. "We'll come to you. Don't leave. And don't come back here until it's safe."

Sam was pulling her out of the house. Everything around them creaked. She knew it wasn't safe for them to stay a moment longer.

"Let's go. I don't want you in there when that tree finally goes through." He quickly moved them through the house and back out the way they came.

Amelia's hand shook in his and her heart raced uncomfortably. She gave Sam's hand a yank once they were outside.

"I need to sit for a second."

He reached for her shoulders. "Are you okay?"

"I'm fine." She took a breath. "I'm fine."

She sat down on the soggy ground and just let it all sink in. Around her she could hear emergency sirens and Sam walked toward the road with his light to let them know the house was empty.

She took in one breath and then another.

So many things raced through her head as she heard the noise of emergency crews. The hysterical cries and loud voices of those who couldn't see what had happened in the dark—who didn't know who might have lived or died.

Her mind wandered from the wet ground she sat on and the noise around her. Had her mother known she was dying all those years ago? She'd never thought much about it until she'd been faced with the firsthand account that people she cared for might have been in that house.

Had her mother's death been sudden, like the storm? Did she think immediately of her family back home, just as Amelia had of Vivian, Penelope, and the girls?

They'd become her family.

Sam had become her family.

She stuck her head between her knees.

Amelia was a strong fighter. She could kill a man with her bare hands, but she couldn't handle what might have been.

Tears began to strain in her throat. Adam had screwed her over and in this very demented way he'd given her two more sisters. Two which she cared about as much as the two she was born to. What would she have done if the family she knew now had been torn apart just as her childhood family had been?

Sam started back to her.

"They want us to leave the area. Are you okay to go?"

She nodded. "We need to go to the house. The old house. They were there."

"Why?"

"I have no idea. We agreed we weren't going to work. We took the night off." She shook her head and looked at him. "Do you think they just knew? I mean—instinct?"

"I don't know." He held out his hand and helped her to her feet. "All I care about is you're okay and so are they. We'll head over."

"God, look at this." She stopped and looked at the house which was in such bad repair to begin with. "They lost their home, Sam. She lost her husband and now she lost her home."

"C'mon. Keep walking. She's going to be fine. I'll call my friend and we'll get her into that townhouse."

Amelia nodded. "That's a good idea."

As they walked through the yard, Sam's arm around her waist, she realized that everything in her life was perfect because of Adam Monroe and his lies. What a strange thing to be thankful for at a moment of pure devastation.

Chapter Twenty-Five

The streets were now full of emergency lights. If you were safe, you were told to stay inside and keep that way. But in a small town, that was just talk. People were going to go to their neighbors and offer help.

Sam pulled the truck up in front of the old house. Candles flickered inside through the windows. Amelia stepped out of the truck and Sam quickly came around the other side to her.

He took her hands in his. "Are you sure you're okay? You were really quiet."

"I'm fine."

"That shook you up back there. I didn't think anything could shake you."

Her lip trembled, but she didn't like that he'd seen her in a weak moment. Worse, he was mentioning it.

"I said I was fine. I just wasn't ready for that. But I'm fine." Her words were sharp.

He nodded. "Okay." Sam kept her hands in his and gave the ring he'd placed on her finger a slight twist. "Leave it to me to make your proposal one you'll never forget, huh?"

"You weren't supposed to propose."

"I know. And I've been a rule follower my whole life. Good thing you did the proposing." He stepped in closer to her. "I shouldn't have been thinking the things I was thinking when we were at your husband's funeral either."

"He never was my husband. A man and wife aren't strangers through their marriage." She moved to him and wrapped her arms around his neck. "I've known you a few months and I feel closer to you than I ever could have imagined with him. You told me you loved me. You bought me a ring." She laughed and held her hand up so she could see it in the dim moonlight, but in her mind it sparkled.

"I do love you. And I'd understand if you took that ring off and shoved it in your pocket. I get it. I understand that."

Amelia pressed her forehead to Sam's. "It's never leaving my finger."

"You're living together," Vivian's voice broke through the dark. "Don't you get enough of this at home?"

Amelia couldn't have imagined there would ever be a day when she was happier to see Vivian Monroe. With Sam guiding them up the steps with his flashlight, Amelia hurried toward the woman in the doorway and pulled her into her arms.

"I was so scared. I've never been scared in my life. Tonight I was scared."

Vivian wrapped her arms around her. "I'm safe. We're all safe. The only tragedy we can see is the front window blew in. I don't know about the roof."

Sam nodded. "I'll look tomorrow."

Amelia pulled back. "I don't think I ever believed in fate. But everything about tonight and the past few months have been all fate."

Vivian began to laugh. "I think something is wrong with you. You sound like Penelope now."

"What does that mean?" Penelope asked from the hallway where she stood with Emma and Ava at her side.

Amelia moved to her quickly and pulled her into her arms. "It means I'm developing a kind and soft side."

"Oh," she said softly.

When she pulled back, Vivian looked at her. "My house is really damaged?"

AMELIA

Amelia looked at Sam and he walked to her side. "I don't know that it will be structurally fixable. That was one big ass tree."

"I told him years ago, when we bought that run down piece of junk, that it needed to come out. Just like everything else, he neglected it."

"You call your insurance company tomorrow," he said resting a hand on Vivian's shoulder. "Tonight we all need to get some rest."

They nodded as the girls each clung to her legs.

"What about my car?" Penelope asked.

"Honey, I don't think it's going to be drivable now. You'll have to turn it in to insurance too."

She frowned in the light of the flashlight. "I don't have insurance. I couldn't afford it."

Amelia closed her eyes tightly trying to figure out one more expense between the three of them when Vivian nudged her.

"Don't you suppose everything had a purpose?" Vivian asked.

"What are you talking about?"

Vivian's teeth were white in the light. "Adam seems to have a car."

Amelia smiled. "You're right." She looked at Penelope. "He does have a car and I personally know it's fully insured because I pay for that."

"Are you kidding me? The Mustang?" Penelope's voice rose in pitch.

"It'll get you to work. Your boss is a tyrant. You won't want to be late," Amelia said.

"You guys." Penelope pulled them both in for a hug and the girls giggled as they hugged legs.

They'd closed up the old house after Amelia and Sam did their best to cover the window. Vivian followed Sam to his house. He had a spare bedroom and a pull out couch. There would be plenty of space for them all for one night.

By the time they'd reached his house, the power was on. Thank goodness they only had a few branches off of trees and patio furniture blown around.

Vivian tucked the girls into the bed upstairs. She left the light on in the hallway and walked back down to the kitchen where Sam was making a pot of water for some tea.

"I hope they fall asleep quickly," Vivian said as she fell into one of the chairs at the kitchen table.

"How did they do in the storm shelter?" Amelia asked as she took down four mugs from the cupboard.

"They acted like they'd been through this a million times. They were calm and followed directions."

"They were calmer than I was," Penelope admitted.

Vivian ran her hands over her face. "I suppose had we been home it would have been a different story."

"Well you weren't. We're just going to be grateful for that," Amelia said setting down the mugs on the table.

"What the hell is that?" Vivian grabbed for her hand as she moved from the cups. "Holy cow, is that what I think it is?"

Amelia whipped her hand back. "Maybe." Oh, she wasn't good with this girlie stuff.

She moved to get away from the wide eyed women at the table, but Sam was right behind her his arms already coming around her from behind.

"Don't get too mushy. She proposed to me," he said.

"You tricked me."

"I navigated the conversation into my direction. I'm a lawyer. That's what I do." He looked at the other women.

"She asked me." He kissed her on the cheek and moved back to the stove when the tea pot began to whistle.

Amelia pursed her lips and gave them all a grunt as she sat down in one of the chairs. "Okay. So, somehow I asked him to marry me and he had a ring under my pillow. So there."

"So you're getting married?" Penelope's grin was brilliant.

"Someday."

"Soon," Sam replied as he walked to the table with the tea pot and set it on a hot pad.

"Soon?" Amelia shot him a look. "You're out of your mind. We have too much going on. We have the house to finish. The business to start. A baby to be born. Vivian's house to tend to."

"That's my business. Not yours," Vivian added as she poured water into her mug.

Amelia narrowed her eyes. "We're a team. I'm here to help you. You can't do it all…"

Vivian held up a finger. "Don't step into my territory." She pulled a tea bag from the holder, opened it, and set it in the water. "Adam isn't here to let me scream and yell at him for leaving the three of us in that house to live. The roof leaked. The plumbing was bad. You saw it. I won't lose much sleep when it's bulldozed to the ground."

Vivian blew a piece of hair from her eyes as she bobbed the tea bag in the water by the string. "I don't care what you all think of me. I'm mad. The S.O.B. didn't give a crap about me or his girls. If he's gone then that house should be too."

She looked up at Amelia. "Don't go hiding that ring or what you think about Sam either. There are only a few of us in this town that even know who you really are. The other day at the store Mrs. Mills told me it was real nice that

Adam's cousins were here helping me out. So there isn't anyone who is going to think you're doing wrong by moving on. That tornado cleansed what I had left of him. Those girls—well they've always been just mine. It's going to stay that way."

Amelia blinked hard and closed her mouth which was open. "You really feel like that? It's not just anger?"

"No. Not just. When your husband is getting married to another woman when you're giving birth to his daughter, you lose a lot of love for him." She shifted her eyes to Sam. "He would never do that to you." She took the tea pouch out of the mug and set it on a paper napkin. "You should marry him soon. It'll be one less Monroe in this town."

That set Amelia into laughter and as usual had the other two following suit. Sam shook his head and sipped his tea. But Amelia knew Vivian was right. One less Mrs. Monroe would certainly keep gossip down.

Mrs. Jackson.

The thought stuck in her head and then shifted to her heart. She could feel her face flush with heat. It was at that moment she realized that even though she'd thought she was in love with Adam she'd never been. Lust—yes. But this was love. That pure stuff you read about in books and saw in movies. Oh, God! She was going to be Mrs. Jackson.

She looked around the table at the other two women talking casually. These women would stand up for her. She was closer in a few months to these two women than she was to her own sisters.

She reached down to her finger and rolled the ring between her fingers. No matter how he'd done it, he'd proposed to her and he'd bought her a ring. He'd given thought to her being his wife. Her! She wasn't domestic. She wasn't even always nice. But he loved her and wanted her forever.

Sam's hand came to her back in such a tender gesture it nearly brought tears to her eyes. He was still in conversation with Vivian, but he was still intimate with her.

Amelia turned to him as he was in mid-sentence, which she'd never heard.

"Is New Year's Day too far away?"

Sam looked at her for a moment. "Too far for what?"

"To get married? Will you marry me on New Year's Day?"

The side of his mouth turned up and there was that dimple. Damn that gorgeous dimple. "Is that what you want?"

"New year. New start. New everything."

Sam reached his hand to her cheek. "New Year's Day it is." He pulled her to him and kissed her ever so gently in front of her new friends.

God, she was happy.

We hope you enjoyed AMELIA, book one in the Three Mrs. Monroes Trilogy.

Here is a preview of book two, PENELOPE.

Available August 2014

Chapter One ~ Penelope

God she was miserable.

Heat waves rose off the pavement and the air was thick and still. Penelope Monroe sat on the front porch in one kitchen chair with her feet up on another. With gentle strokes, she rubbed her pregnant belly. She simply couldn't believe how uncomfortable she was.

The smell of paint from inside the house wafted out and she tried not to let it make her stomach churn. She'd been appointed to oversee the two men putting in the new front window. That wasn't much fun at all.

Both of their butt cracks stuck out of their pants and every time they talked they cursed then looked at her and apologized. She wasn't a prude—well not really. She'd heard those words before, even if she didn't use them.

Penelope closed her eyes and wished for a slight breeze. Her head was buzzing with paint fumes, curse words, and the events of the past few months.

It had all started when she'd married Adam Monroe.

His image formed in her head and she let out a small sigh.

Those blue eyes and that blonde hair, he was like a god, she thought. One she'd read about in books. He was a Marine, so his body was chiseled hard and he carried himself—well, like a god.

He'd been a player. She'd known that. The night she'd first laid eyes on him, he'd taken her friend home from the bar. At least he'd had the sense to offer her a ride home before he drove off with Christina—her *ex-friend*. There were explicit details from Christina she could do with forgetting.

PENELOPE

That should have been her clue to never even talk to the man again. Easy sex from women you picked up in bars wasn't her style. She'd been a virgin, after all. She'd been saving herself for her husband. It had been Christina who thought differently of that. Christina liked the loud music, the dancing, the beer, and the men. Usually she was considerate of Penelope's feelings when they went out. But that night Christina had gotten caught up in Adam's blue eyes, his hair, his body, and his voice delivering all the right lines.

Penelope figured she was most mad about the evening because she'd been having feelings she'd never had before. She thought, briefly, that had she been given the chance to go home with Adam she'd have done it. She knew she'd have chickened out, but he'd had a way with turning her heart to mush.

But it had been Christina he'd taken back to his place and—well, again, she'd just like to forget that she knew every detail of that night.

She couldn't have imagined that a few nights later, when Christina had abandoned her at the bar for another one night stand, that Adam would walk in and change her life.

The words he used were different than the ones he'd used on Christina. His moves were gentle and that hadn't been a word Christina had used when she'd given Penelope all of her details.

He was a gentleman.

They talked, walked, and dated a few nights. He was sweet when she told him she was a virgin and she was saving herself for her husband. Not once did he make a move or cross a line. Then he said he loved her and that had changed everything.

When he'd asked her to marry him, there had been no hesitation. They'd gotten married and, that night, she gave herself to him.

Penelope let out a breath and opened her eyes. Everything changed in that one night.

She ran her hand over her growing stomach. A small part of Adam grew inside of her, even though he was gone.

The day she'd come to Parson's Gulch was the day they'd buried Adam—the day she'd met one of his other wives and seen the other with his children. She was only one of three Mrs. Monroes. One of three Adam had lied to. One of three who now fought to move past him.

The very thought of Adam's lies still made her sick.

But just because she now detested her husband of only a few months, she couldn't hate the life that grew inside of her. This child was hers and in a few days she'd see the baby for the first time. Adam's other wives would be there too.

She let out a small chuckle which had the window installers looking over at her. Kindly, she gave them a smile and closed her eyes again.

Amelia Monroe, Adam's second wife, had taken her in. She was kind though Penelope was sure she wasn't used to being so kind But she'd given her a place to stay and had just friended her when she'd needed someone to care.

Vivian, on the other hand, had taken a little longer to warm up to. But when she had, they'd bonded. Though Vivian wasn't more than ten years older than Penelope, she thought of her as a mother figure, where Amelia was more of a big sister.

Adam's lies had entangled them.

Adam's death had brought them together.

Adam's life grew inside of her.

Penelope opened her eyes and rubbed her aching side.

In just the past week, her stomach had grown so much bigger. It stretched and Vivian was relentless with the cocoa butter routine. She had stretch marks from Adam's other two children and she was going to make sure Penelope didn't suffer the same fate.

More than just her stomach had changed though. A week ago, the entire town changed in fifteen seconds when a tornado ripped through the sky. There had only been a few injuries and no one had died—thank God!

Vivian's home had been totaled and the front window of the century-old house on Main and Pine had blown in. Penelope's car had also been totaled, but she thought she'd faired pretty well in that deal. Her beat up old car, which didn't always run well, had been replaced by her late husband's vintage Mustang.

Penelope had never been one for flashy, vintage cars, but she couldn't help herself—she loved this one. It sat against the curb within view. Oh, she might look sexy in it now, from the neck up. But no one would ever give her a second look when they saw a baby seat in the back in a few months.

Sam Jackson, Adam's lawyer, her boss, and now Amelia's fiancé, pulled tree branches around the side of the house and stacked them near the porch.

"I have the misting fan set up in the kitchen. Maybe you should go inside," he called to her.

"Too much paint."

He nodded as he took his cellphone out of his pocket. He looked at it, smiled, and walked toward her giving the front window a glance first. "Why don't you go in, get yourself a cold bottle of water, and walk upstairs."

Penelope frowned. She knew it was much hotter upstairs.

Sam climbed the steps of the porch and held his hand out to her. "C'mon. Amelia is up there. She just texted me. She has something to show you."

Penelope planted her feet on the floor, took Sam's hand, and stood with an *umph*.

"You start up," he said placing his hand on her back and walking her toward the door. "I'll get you a bottle of water and meet you up there."

Penelope shifted him a glance and walked inside the house.

The heat was nearly unbearable, but she walked toward the stairs and started up them.

Sam had redone every tread and in time, when she wasn't around, they would stain them and the rest of the floors in the century-old house, which they were turning into a daycare center.

Adam's father had donated the house to them. It was a kind gesture, she thought as she neared the top step. He'd been gracious when they'd needed it.

Amelia had come up with the great idea that they take what Adam had and turn it into a business to take care of his children. Amelia hadn't asked for anything in return. But when pushed, she'd mentioned she'd like a gym in the basement.

So far she hadn't stumbled across the secret project Penelope and Vivian had been working on. She seemed to be preoccupied with what she was calling her office upstairs.

Penelope hadn't been upstairs in weeks. It wasn't worth the climb. And now that she was at the top of the stairs and the air was thick and horribly hot, she knew she'd been right to stay downstairs.

Sam was right behind her with a cold bottle of water. He handed it to her.

232

"C'mon, go in," he said.

"She's been behind those doors for a week. I don't want to be the one who goes in unannounced."

"You're chicken."

"Yeah. You go first. She loves you."

Sam scowled and stepped forward. "Yeah, and I'm the one she punched in the gut when I startled her too. I'm walking with heavy footsteps."

He twisted the knob of one of the closed bedroom doors and pushed it open. Sticking his head around the corner, he pushed it open just a bit more.

"She's afraid to come in. You're not going to throw anything are you?"

Penelope heard Amelia grunt and then the door swung open hard. "Get in here."

Penelope walked through the thick air toward the room and gasped when she walked in.

Amelia, Vivian, and Vivian's daughters were standing in the room with enormous grins on their faces. "Well, what do you think?"

Penelope looked around at the transformed area. They had taken the two bedrooms, which shared a Jack and Jill bathroom, and completely renovated them.

The room she stood in was painted a very soothing shade of pale green. There was a wrought iron bed with a lacy white spread. Over the bed, was a painting that she knew Vivian had found in the basement. An antique dresser and mirror sat against the wall and they'd also added a beautiful armoire.

"This is magnificent," she said with her breath wheezing out. "This is what you've been working on?"

"Yes. You needed a place to stay," Vivian said. "Amelia did almost all of it."

"For me?"

"You and the baby. This is your home now—when the fumes are all gone."

She felt the tears sting, but she tried to hold them back.

"I did that." Emma, Vivian's four year old daughter said as she pointed to the rocking chair. "The Teddy bear. I made it at Build-a-Bear."

Penelope covered her mouth and tears quickly rolled down her cheeks.

"You're such a girl," Amelia teased as she put her arm around Penelope's shoulders. "C'mon, there's more. Try not to cry too much or you won't be able to see anything."

She walked her to the bathroom that joined the two rooms. It was painted a soft brown and all the fixtures had been replaced with modern replicas of older ones.

"This is gorgeous. I can't believe I didn't know you were doing this."

"That would have ruined the surprise. Okay, now you can cry your eyes out," Amelia said as she opened the door that led into the next bedroom."

When Penelope saw it, she did cry harder. The pastel yellow room with handmade curtains depicting tumbling teddy bears hung from the window. Matching bumpers adorned a crib against the wall. There was a matching rocking chair in this room with a teddy bear on the seat.

Ava, Vivian's two-year-old, tugged on Penelope's shirt. "I made that."

Penelope batted her eyes and ran her hand over Ava's braids and smiled. Never in her life could she have expected such love. And to think, these women and children had been jaded by Adam's lies too. But they were there for her and her baby. They embraced her. They loved her.

"I can't...I don't...Oh..." she sobbed.

Vivian moved to Penelope and wrapped her arms around her. "Quit crying. You're going to make me cry."

"I don't deserve this," Penelope said.

"Sure you do," Amelia added.

Penelope looked up to see her standing with her arms crossed over her chest and Sam next to her with his arm around her shoulders. They made a beautiful picture, she thought. Amelia was very lucky to have fallen in love with him.

"You've all been so nice to me..."

"And we're going to keep being nice." Amelia walked toward her and whispered, "Adam brought us together. We are all family now." She took Penelope's hands in hers. "This is the least he could do to take care of you and your baby."

Again, Amelia was being sweet and that nearly made Penelope want to laugh. But she'd learned this side of Amelia was as genuine as the side that liked to kick men's butts.

As Ava and Emma showed Penelope all the parts to *their baby's* room, the doorbell rang.

They all exchanged glances and Vivian shook her head. "I'll get it. It's probably those boobs putting in the window."

Penelope watched her walk out of the room and then, hand in hand, Sam and Amelia walked out too. She looked down at the sisters of her baby and smiled. She'd be okay without Adam there or any other man for that matter. She and her baby were loved. That's all that mattered.

Meet the Author

Damon Kappel ©2009

Bestselling Author Bernadette Marie is known for building families readers want to be part of. Her series *The Keller Family* has graced bestseller charts since its release in 2011, along with her other series and single title books. The married mother of five sons promises *Happily Ever After always*...and says she can write it, because she lives it.

When not writing, Bernadette Marie is shuffling her sons to their many events—mostly hockey—and enjoying the beautiful views of the Colorado Rocky Mountains from her front step. She is also an accomplished martial artist with a second degree black belt in Tang Soo Do.

A chronic entrepreneur, Bernadette Marie opened her own publishing house in 2011, *5 Prince Publishing*, so that she could publish the books she liked to write and help make the dreams of other aspiring authors come true too.

5 Prince Publishing is proud to present *The Letter Drawer* by Sarah Galloway. Please enjoy this excerpt. You can find this book and many more on the 5 Prince Publishing site at www.5princebooks.com

The Letter Drawer
By
Sarah Galloway

1 ~ The Letter Drawer

They had been so young, so very young. She remembered walking to the school bus, alone and scared. Her first day of first grade and then there he was, a young boy in a dress shirt and slacks, a lunch box in his hand and a blue and red backpack on his back. Tall and quiet, the boy's eyes did not meet hers. His dark brown hair was well cropped above his big brown eyes. She saw him and lost some of her fear. Walking up next to him, she stood silently as they waited for the bus.

That was the beginning of it. From that moment on, they were never far from one another. She chose a seat next to him in class and she always picked the seat next to him on the bus ride home. They sat in silence at first, both looking straight ahead with their hands folded neatly in their lap.

Later, when she could finally stand the silence no more, she glanced over at him. "My name is Claire, what's yours?"

The boy's voice was quiet. "Evan."

"Evan," she repeated softly. "Okay."

He gave her a puzzled look. "Okay what?"

"Okay, I like your name Evan. You can be my friend."

Evan looked at her, a small, confused smile playing at the corner of his lips.

Time went on. They played, built forts, explored the forest behind their neighborhood, and laughed. They grew up together. They became best friends, and that did not change.

Middle school approached and Evan became an awkward, lanky boy while Claire was a dark-haired, green-eyed beauty. She didn't seem to care. All of the sudden, the boys noticed Claire, but still, she stayed by Evan.

"Hey Claire," they would say. "Want to come hang out with us after school?"

"No thanks," replied Claire.

"Why not?"

"I'm studying with Evan."

Despite the whispering, whining, and complaining that came from the other boys, Claire never wavered. When she left school, she always walked to the bus with Evan. She rode with him, laughed, and told jokes with him, even when the others snickered or sneered.

One day, as they rode next to each other, Claire realized that what she felt for Evan was more than just friendship. She reached over and took his strong, masculine hand, clasping it in her own much smaller one. He looked up at her, waiting for something.

Wondering what was on her mind, he interrupted the silence. "Claire?"

"Yes, Evan?"

Brown eyes sparkled back at her. "Are you okay?"

"Yes, Evan."

The gaze lasted a moment longer. "Are you sure?"

"Yes, Evan."

He left his hand sandwiched between hers. "Alright then."

When the bus came to a stop, Claire stood and waited for Evan to stand beside her and they walked off together, as they always did.

Standing there on the sidewalk, Claire silently stared at Evan, not moving.

Evan was clearly confused. "Ummm, did you want to come over and study?"

"Not really."

Absently, he scratched the top of his head. "Alright then. I'll see you tomorrow?"

"No." She halted him with her hand on his shoulder. "Come with me."

Pausing for a moment, he gave her an inquiring look. "Where are we going?"

She clasped his hand in hers. "Just come."

They were seventeen and when she took his hand this time, it was because she loved him. She led him into the forest and back through trees they hadn't been under in years. They walked through the thick underbrush and finally came to a clearing. He looked at it and smiled. A couple of old, beat-up pieces of plywood leaned together were held there by nails creating a sanctuary fashioned by children. Various odd blankets and pieces of bark and wood that were tattered and faded and barely recognizable lay underneath them.

Confused, he glanced from her to their favorite childhood place. "Claire, this is our old fort."

She pulled him toward it. "Yes."

"I had forgotten about this place."

The light breeze rushed through her hair. "Do you remember when we built it?"

Nostalgia was obvious on his features. "Of course I do! Oh gosh, how old were we, nine, ten maybe?"

"We were in third grade. It was fun. Come and sit with me under it now, will you?"

As she pulled him forward, he laughed. "Okay Claire."

On their hands and knees, the dusty ground was cool and soft as they crawled into the tattered old fort. When they were sitting under it, there was barely enough room for both of them and Evan's body was cramped against Claire's so that they would fit.

Claire smiled at Evan and touched his forehead, brushing a lock of fallen hair away from his eyes.

A serious expression fell across his face. "Claire, can I ask you something?"

"Of course."

Evan's eyes trailed off to the horizon. "Why do you still stay with me?"

"What do you mean?"

He shifted his gaze back to her. "I mean, you're ... well, you're beautiful Claire. All those guys want to be with you, the good looking ones, the ones all the girls want to be with, and you still always hang out with me."

"Well," said Claire blushing. "That's part of what I wanted to talk to you about."

"What is?"

Unblinking eyes stared back at her as she spoke. "Evan, I think I'm in love with you."

A friendly bear hug enveloped her. "I love you too, Claire."

"No, you don't understand. Not like a friend, not like we are best friends. I think I have fallen in love with you."

He looked at her, as though he was barely registering what she was saying. She looked back into his dark brown eyes. Still, he said nothing. Finally, she leaned forward and kissed him on the lips. It was a soft and tender kiss, yet it was warm and inviting, too. And it was perfect, like they had done it all of their lives.

The words fell out of her mouth in a whisper. "Evan, I mean it. I love you."

His voice was soft and tender. "Oh Claire, I love you too."

Now he put his arms around her and she rested her head on his shoulder, feeling the warmth of his body. They stayed that way, he held her and she curled up within his arms, finally able to relax now that she knew that he loved her too.

That had been twenty years ago.

Claire thought back on the memory and smiled. *Twenty years. Has it really been that long?* Twenty years since she realized that she truly did love Evan. *It seems like only yesterday.*

She closed her eyes and pictured him as he looked now. Sharp jaw, strong features, tall and lean and handsome. Evan was the kind of guy that women looked at twice when he walked by, although he didn't realize it. Those soft, gentle brown eyes that she loved and adored still made her feel weak and he still had the shock of deep brown hair that he had to trim constantly because it grew so quickly.

He had been such a scrawny kid that nobody understood why she went for him when she could have any boy in the school, had she wanted them. They simply didn't understand love. She had belonged to Evan from the first time she saw him. She had always been his.

Evan had taken more convincing. It wasn't that he didn't love Claire, because he did. It was more that he was terrified of her. He was scared to death that she would realize how amazing she was and that she would go fleeting off into the arms of one of the rough looking muscled guys that were always hitting on her. Eventually though, he realized that she only saw him and he began to feel safe with her. In time he learned that they truly did belong together and that she would never leave him. He didn't quite understand why, but he knew it to be true all the same.

Claire closed her eyes and pictured Evan next to her. She could almost feel his breath on her skin. But it was too soon, he wouldn't be home for another five months. Sighing, she forced herself up to make breakfast.

Claire pulled the contents from her cupboard to make pancakes and began mixing the batter. As she was holding the bowl under one arm and whisking with the other, she heard Eve's soft footsteps on the linoleum. The quiet, dainty sound of Eve's feet were soon overshadowed by Connor's much louder thuds.

Her two children came into the kitchen, both still half-asleep. Seventeen-year-old Connor was in sweatpants and a t-shirt, while thirteen-year-old Eve stood in a long night shirt and knit sleep pants.

Claire greeted them warmly. "Good morning kids."

"Mmmph," groaned Connor.

Eve yawned. "Morning."

"Oh come on now you two, it's a beautiful day, just look outside."

They both looked out the window, indifference on their faces.

Jackson, the family pet, came meandering into the kitchen when he heard the kids. The huge, black Great Dane pressed himself against Connor.

"Ooooph." The air rushed out of Connor. "Jackson, it's too early."

The dog quite happily moseyed away to Eve who patted him lightly on the head. Then he walked to Claire and sat down next to her. She leaned playfully on him while she waited for the pancake in the skillet to be ready to flip, he didn't budge.

Connor got out the milk and poured himself a glass. "Do you want some Eve? Mom?"

"Yeah," yawned Eve as she took her place at the table, wiping sleep from her eyes.

Claire flipped a pancake in the skillet. "No thank you honey."

Connor poured a second glass and walked it to Eve who took it, thanked him and sipped at it as she tried to will herself awake. Claire finished cooking breakfast and put some on the plates, handing them to the kids. She watched as Connor carefully poured syrup onto each pancake and then handed the bottle to his sister. Eve cut up her pancakes with a fork first, and then lathered syrup all over the small fragments.

Eve handed the bottle to her Mom. Claire put a tiny dollop of syrup on her single pancake and then spread it across in a thin, even layer. She smiled as she watched the kids eat. Slowly, they began to wake up.

Connor finished first, his voice still hazy. "I'm gonna shower."

"Okay," said Claire.

Connor left and Eve sat at the table with her daughter.

There was silence before Eve finally spoke. "Mom?"

"Yeah?"

"I miss Dad."

Claire sighed. "So do I. Five more months and he'll be home."

Eve's face drooped. "It's still so long."

Claire's heart ached as she looked across the table at her daughter. "I know honey. I miss him too. Soon, soon he will be home."

Eve looked up at her mother with solemn eyes. "Can he stay this time?"

Patting her daughter's hand, she spoke. "I hope so honey."

"Me too."

Eve's young face flushed and Claire could tell she was holding back tears. Claire opened her arms and Eve walked to her mother and hugged her. Claire held her daughter and silently thanked God that, unlike most thirteen year olds, Eve still let her comfort her this way. She stroked Eve's dark brown hair until she finally let go.

Her daughter's eyes looked moist, but she no longer looked as though she would begin to cry. "Are you okay honey?"

"Yeah, it's just one of those days I guess. I'm gonna get ready."

She watched Eve disappear down the hallway to her room. Alone in the kitchen, Claire began picking up plates and putting them in the sink. She heard the shower stop and a few minutes later, Connor emerged looking much more like the bright, chipper boy that he was. *He takes after his father so much.* He was tall and lean, just like Evan, and he had those same deep brown eyes. Claire smiled at him and he returned the grin.

As she finished rinsing the dishes, she looked over at him. "Connor?"

He slung his backpack over his shoulder. "Yeah?"

"Would you mind dropping Eve off at school this morning? I am going to write your father a letter."

His free arm wrapped around her shoulder and hugged her. "Sure Mom."

"Thanks honey."

"You're welcome."

He was such a good boy. They were both good kids. She was so thankful for them. "C'mon   Eve,"   Connor called from the kitchen. "Five minutes."

Eve's voice trailed in from her bedroom. "Okay, I'll be there."

Just in time, Eve appeared with her book bag slung over her shoulder and Connor walked with her to the door. Eve looked as though she were a little less sad and Claire felt relieved.

Claire lifted her hand to wave goodbye to her children. "Have a good day guys."

"We will Mom," replied Eve. "Love you."

"Love you," chimed Connor.

Her heart swelled with joy. "I love you both, too." Her children were so good to her. She watched out the window as they climbed into Connor's old but reliable car, laughing about something. Then she returned to the nook.

As they pulled away, Claire sat in the warm light that shone through the window onto the breakfast table. The glossy surface was cool against her wrists, but the sun was warm on her back. She brushed her hair back with her hands, feeling the soft curls run through her fingers. Retrieving a piece of paper from the little drawer hidden under the surface of the table, Claire began to write.

My Dearest Evan...

Claire wrote the letter, telling him everything that was in her heart. She read it over. When she was satisfied that she had said everything that she needed to say, she signed it:

Your wife,
Claire

She placed a red lipstick kiss at the corner of it by her name. She slipped the letter into an envelope and addressed it to the APO address where the Army would receive the mail before dispensing it to the soldiers.

THE LETTER DRAWER

She closed her eyes for a moment, holding the letter in her hand and feeling the sun on her back. In that moment, she felt at peace. Her white, gauzy nightgown flowed softly in the ruffle of the breeze coming in through the window. It brushed against her thigh and then floated away as quickly as a whisper. Her hair fluttered against her face and she closed her eyes, embracing the wind. As she opened her eyes and rose, she felt the sun's rays leave her back. Placing the letter on the edge of the kitchen counter, she walked to the bedroom. As she slipped into a pair of jeans, she retrieved a lemon yellow blouse that was well fitted to her figure. She could almost hear Evan telling her how beautiful she was and how he could get lost in her eyes forever. Moving back to the kitchen, she paused to pick up her car keys. She glanced at the letter before deciding she would place it in the outgoing mail in the afternoon. When she climbed into her car, a soft smile rested gently on her lips.

That was the last time Claire's family ever saw her alive.

Books from 5 Prince Publishing
www.5princebooks.com

THE LETTER DRAWER

Encore *Bernadette Marie*
Split Decisions *Carmen DeSousa*
Matchmakers *Bernadette Marie*
Rocky Road *Susan Lohrer*
Stutter Creek *Ann Swann*
The Perfect Crime *P. Hindley, S. Goodsell*
Lost and Found *Bernadette Marie*
A Heart at Home *Sara Barnard*
Soul Connection *Doug Simpson*
Bridge Over the Atlantic *Lisa Hobman*
Unexpected Admirer *Bernadette Marie*
Jaded *M.J. Kane*
Shades of Darkness *Melynda Price*
Heart like an Ocean *Christine Steendam*
The Depot *Carmen DeSousa*
Crisis of Identity *Denise Moncrief*
A Heart Broken *Sara Barnard*
Soul Mind *Doug Simpson*
Chunky Sugars *Sara Barnard*
When Noon day Ends *Carmen DeSousa*
Fatal Jealousy *Christina OW*
Center Stage *Bernadette Marie*
Chris Mouse and the Promise *Tina J Adams*
Soul Rescue *Doug Simpson*
The Pit Stop *Carmen DeSousa*
Soul Awakening *Doug Simpson*
First Kiss *Bernadette Marie*
A Heart Not Easily Broken *MJ Kane*
Entangled Dreams *Carmen DeSousa*
All for Love *Ann Swann*